PRAISE FOR CB SAMET

Four-time award winning author

GRAY HORIZON: 2019 Readers' Favorite Bronze Winner in Thriller category

MASTERS FILE: 2018 Readers' Favorite Honorable Mention in Romantic Suspense category

THE AVANT CHAMPION ~RISING~: 2017 EVVY Award 2nd Place in Fantasy category and 2018 Great Southeastern Book Festival Honorable Mention in Fantasy

"CB Samet is a master of the craft."

— READERS' FAVORITE REVIEWER ON WHYTE KNIGHT

MALTISSE FILE

THE RIDER FILES BOOK 4

CB SAMET

NOVELS BY CB SAMET

Cover Art by Circe Corp

e-book ISBN: 978-1-950942-00-8

print ISBN: 978-1-950942-01-5

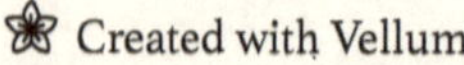 Created with Vellum

1

*D*rake lifted the limp Bullmastiff off the kitchen floor. Bending with his knees, he cradled the animal in his arms. He strained to carry the gargantuan animal to his car.

What had he done? He was a dead man for sure.

When Drake reached his Explorer, he loaded the animal into the back of his vehicle. Despite the cool temperature of this winter day in Atlanta, sweat drenched his face and shirt. The perspiration wasn't from carrying the beast alone. The fear surging through his body contributed significantly.

Drake's phone rang through his Bluetooth earpiece. He accepted the call from his friend, Peter Bower.

"Hey, Pete." Drake leaned his back against his Explorer, catching his breath.

"Hey, man. How's undercover security work going?" Pete's voice sounded cheerful—a stark contrast to the dread Drake felt.

"Not good." Drake glanced nervously around his surroundings.

"Oh? What's wrong?"

"Claire's been kidnapped." Drake ran a hand through the dog's coarse black, brown hair. He'd never petted the dog before—he'd never been this close to it. "It's my fault."

"Claire? As in the girl you were assigned to investigate? I thought you were reassigned."

Drake closed the hatch. "Yes, and yes. I was assigned to get close to her and learn her patterns—maybe plant spyware—but I failed. Her lie detector of a dog made her suspicious of me."

Drake glanced through the window at the sleeping monstrosity. The Bullmastiff looked like a big, stuffed animal instead of the protective, trained beast he was.

"Then, I was reassigned."

Although he'd been reassigned, Drake had still pursued Claire—under some foolish desire for a real relationship.

"So, what's the kidnapping got to do with you?"

Drake remembered his horror, thirty minutes earlier—when he'd overheard one of Titan's men mention Claire's kidnapping. He'd seen her just yesterday—he'd thought she *might* still be at her place. Maybe they hadn't gotten to her yet.

But when Drake had raced over to her house, she was already gone—and Bear lay unconscious on the floor of her bedroom.

"If I'd succeeded in my assignment, Titan Enterprises wouldn't have resorted to such extreme measures in kidnapping her."

"Man, this does *not* sound like anything you need to get mixed up in, Drake. What the hell kind of security agency kidnaps people?"

The bad kind, Drake thought. The kind of agency who had no qualms about killing people, either.

Drake rubbed his temple. When had everything spiraled out of control?

"I have to find her." Drake climbed into his Explorer, buckled in, and started the engine.

"May I remind you that you don't belong with these people?" Pete warned. "You're not even one of them."

"True—but I still have to fix this."

"You're an actor, Drake. You're not former military, like these guys. This sounds like a suicide mission."

"Thanks for the vote of confidence." Drake pulled away from the curb and headed north, out of Claire's neighborhood.

"Someone needs to point out the obvious to you."

"Well, *obviously* I'm going to have to demonstrate some badass acting skills to pull this off."

"Does this mean bro weekend is a no go?"

"Ah. Dang it." Drake suppressed a groan. "Sorry, Pete." He'd forgotten he'd invited Pete to stay with him. "Where are you now?"

"Just landed at Hartsfield International. I was going to ride-share to your place. I brought the Xbox."

"Change of plans."

"No! Hell, no. I'm not getting involved in your crap."

"You can't go to my place, Pete. When they find out I'm helping Claire, Titan's men will come for me."

"I'll get a hotel room."

"I need a getaway driver."

CLAIRE SHIFTED her weight in the hard, wooden chair. Straight, stringy blue strands of hair fell across her face. Her body ached from being bound in the same position for hours. Her wrists were raw from the plastic ties securing her to the arms of the chair. The throbbing in her temple was escalating to a relentless pounding.

She suspected the pain originated from hitting her head on her kitchen floor when the asshole had hit her with a stun gun. Claire realized she had rug burns on her shoulder, too—which must have occurred when they'd thrown her into the trunk. That was where she'd woken up, just before they'd hauled her into this cabin and tied her to the chair.

Maxine Rider was going to kill them.

Claire's boss—a former Marine—would tear her abductors to shreds when she found Claire; and that was only if Mica McMillan, Claire's martial arts expert friend, didn't beat Maxine to it. Then there was Ranger Ryan Walsh—who was like an older brother to Claire. Her abductors could only hope *he* didn't get his hands on them first.

Oh, yes—Claire had powerful friends. These kidnappers—Titan's men—had just messed with the wrong woman.

The problem was that her team wouldn't know where to find her. Maxine could track Claire's phone or smart watch, but Claire had neither of those on her. Lucius Titan was too smart to have this remote cabin linked to his name. No one would be able to track her here.

Claire's options were to escape or wait for rescue. She tugged against the twist ties on her wrists. They didn't budge.

Rescue it is, then.

She shivered from the chill in the room. Spending the night in an old cabin—without central heating, in February, in the North Georgia mountains—felt like she'd been tied up in the back of a refrigerator. Assuming Claire *was* in the North Georgia mountains, that is—although judging by the drive time and elevation, she had to be in either North Georgia or South Carolina.

Aside from fearing if the Rider team would find this place before Titan's men killed her, Claire was worried her kidnappers would torture valuable information about Rider Security and

Investigation out of her. After all, that must be the reason they'd abducted her—she was the company's information specialist.

The only other reason would be to lure Maxine and the Rider team into a trap—but Claire knew that Max was way too smart to fall for any traps.

Damn Drake.

Claire had trusted him—she'd even been moronically close to losing her heart to him. Manipulative prick. She'd believed Drake had been who he'd claimed to be—an actor and stunt double—because her cursory background check confirmed his story; but *of course* a Titan employee would have an excellent cover story, and he'd even fooled her.

Well, he *had*—right up until she'd found a Titan business card in his wallet. Rookie mistake on Drake's part.

Claire hadn't been snooping. He'd asked her to pull out his bankcard, so he could pick up cash for their movie date—but they hadn't made it to the movies.

Claire had stared at the card in disbelief when she'd stumbled across it. Why would Drake have a business card belonging to the Rider team's arch nemesis?

When she'd turned to glare at him, the '*oh, shit*' look in Drake's eyes had been all the confession she'd needed. Claire promptly exited his Explorer—right there at the bank—and caught a ride-share home.

Through her angry tears, she hadn't noticed the car parked on the curb—just one house down from her address. However, when Claire unlocked her front door and Bear hadn't immediately rushed to greet her, her body went cold and her senses hit high alert.

That was also when the kidnappers hit her with what felt like a million volts of electricity.

Bear.

As she sat bound to that chair, tears welled in Claire's eyes. Her dog would never have let the attackers take her, which meant they had to have killed poor Bear. Heart wrenching fury pounded through her.

MAXINE BEGAN to roll out of bed when strong arms wrapped around her.

"Don't go," said the deep voice, in its distinctive Russian accent.

"I'm already late for work," Maxine replied.

With a reluctant moan, Vladimir loosened his hold on her. "But you own the business, *dorogoy*," he protested sweetly.

"And I wouldn't set much of an example for my staff and my clients if I'm late for work." Maxine slid out of his embrace. She walked to the bathroom where she freshened up before dressing in cargo pants and a cotton shirt.

When she emerged from the bedroom and into the kitchen, Vladimir was waiting for her. He handed Maxine a cup of coffee, while she blinked at the shirtless man.

At some point, she'd have to get used to his presence in her life. Vladimir was making an effort to be in town for the entire month to spend time with her. Last month, he'd been gone—working in St. Petersburg, an entire ocean away. She hadn't admitted to him how much she'd missed him.

Maxine murmured a 'thank you' as she drank her coffee and collected her belongings.

Vladimir didn't need to know she missed him in his absence. He'd eased into her life like smooth Belvedere Vodka—you didn't know you'd consumed too much until it was too late. Vladimir hadn't intoxicated her; he'd just given her slow, steady doses until she was addicted. Maxine thought about him when he was gone. She looked forward to seeing him when he came back. Her desire for him extended beyond the physical. While the amazing intimacy stole her breath and curled her toes, she enjoyed his humor and his compassion equally as much.

Maxine patted her pockets. "I need my..."

At the end of Vladimir's outstretched arm was the phone she was about to start looking for.

Maxine stood on her tiptoes and kissed his cheek. "Thanks."

Even after spending all this time with Vladimir, Maxine was still surprised by the thoughtfulness and kindness this man possessed. No one who knew Vladimir Pronin as the leader of the Russian Mafia would believe the depths of his soul—or how he'd bared it to her. Was it his vulnerability she'd fallen in love with?

After bidding Vladimir farewell, Maxine got into her Crossover and drove through Atlanta to work. She arrived at the Rider SI building and took the elevator to the third floor. In the reception area, a ficus plant separated two, cushioned chairs—which both faced a check-in-desk. The desk was chest-high and made of curved oak, behind which hung an illuminated sign: Rider Security and Investigation. The motion-activated secretary hologram flickered on behind the desk with a silky automated greeting: "Welcome to the offices of Rider Security and Investigation. Please sign in on the electronic tablet and..."

Maxine walked straight past the hologram and entered her passcode which unlocked the door to the company office. She continued down the hallway as the hologram automatically turned off, since no one had checked-in at the kiosk.

Maxine stopped at Claire's office. Her computers were off, as well as her flickering LED fairy lights. The room was quiescent and unoccupied.

Maxine's eye twitched. Claire was never late to work—and if she'd planned to work from home, she would've texted Maxine to let her know. Maxine pulled her phone from the pocket of her cargo pants. No messages.

Next, she called Claire—but the call went unanswered, straight to voicemail. A tense knot formed in Maxine's stomach.

She walked to her office and powered on her computer. The wait felt interminable, but for security purposes, Claire had Maxine shut down all work computers at the end of each day. At last, Maxine logged in and pulled up the program to locate Claire's phone.

She entered another password and selected Claire from a list of all her employees. They each had one phone Maxine could trace and one untraceable phone. Claire's phone showed she was at her home. Maxine's information specialist didn't have a landline she could call, so she'd have to make a trip to Claire's house.

As Maxine left her office, she dialed the number for Mica McMillan. Mica was one of Maxine's newer employees, who currently provided undercover protection and enhanced security services to weapons manufacturer Bill Sharp.

"Max. What's up?"

"When was your last contact with Claire?"

"Two nights ago. We had Mexican at Taco Veloz. Is something wrong?"

"Could be nothing. Could be I'm just on edge after we took down AJ Schlau."

With Mica's help, the Rider SI team had apprehended one of Lucius's top scumbags. They'd turned him over to the FBI, along with incriminating evidence of drug dealing and trafficking women. Unfortunately, none of those illegal activities could be traced back to Lucius.

Nevertheless, the blow to Titan Enterprises—not to mention the personal insult to Lucius, at having lost one of his criminal masterminds—could have resulted in retaliation. The worry of his involvement kept Maxine hyper alert.

"Something got you concerned, Max? What do you need me to do?" Mica asked.

Mica and Claire had developed a friendship in the short months since Mica had been hired, and Maxine had observed both women were the better for it.

"For now, nothing." Maxine exited the elevator and walked through the parking garage to her silver Crossover. "I'm heading to Claire's house—where her phone is located. I'll see if she's there."

"Text me as soon as you know she's safe."

"Copy that." Maxine hung up the phone.

She drove her SUV with determined focus, pushing the speed limit to reach Claire's house. On the way, she tried to reassure herself that Claire could simply be at home; perhaps sick with the flu, or maybe she slept in late with that guy she was seeing—Fitzy.

Was Claire still seeing him? Did Fitzy know where Claire was?

That wasn't his real name. Fitzy had been the nickname Maxine used to tease Claire. She'd never met the man, but Claire had told her he was an actor. What even was his real name? Then, it came to her.

Drake Fitzgerald.

But if he and Claire were spending the morning together, Claire could still damn well answer her phone. If Maxine turned up at Claire's place and intruded on something intimate, it would be Claire's own fault for not answering her phone.

But even as Maxine tried to reassure herself, the hair on the back of her neck stood on end, and her senses flashed with warnings—like a strobe light. She pulled her Sig Sauer from the glove compartment and lay it on the passenger seat.

Finally, Maxine pulled into Claire's driveway. She cut the engine and her feet hit the ground at a trot. She ignored the protesting ache in her arthritic knee.

The door to Claire's one-story, three-bedroom house was slightly ajar. Maxine scanned the perimeter. There were no other vehicles and no one on the grounds.

Maxine pushed past the hinged gate, hanging from a

picturesque, white picket fence. She walked through Claire's yard, past the tiny buds on the azaleas in early bloom. Cautiously, Maxine approached the house.

Nothing around the exterior appeared out of order. All was quiet.

"Claire?"

As Maxine called out, she pressed herself against one wall—positioned beside the front door with her gun in her hand.

No one answered. More significantly, Bear didn't bark or show himself. The enormous Bullmastiff was highly protective of Claire. Where was he? His absence only escalated Maxine's anxiety.

She stepped through the doorway, leading with her weapon. Cautiously, Maxine swept the house. She found Claire's phone on the floor of the kitchen—the screen cracked. The battery was also dead. Ice cold talons of dread wrapped around Maxine's chest and squeezed up into her throat.

2

ica McMillan received an alarming follow-up text from Maxine: *Claire's been kidnapped.*

Mica left her workstation and barged into Bill Sharp's office.

Bill's eyes opened wide with alarm. "Mica?"

"Claire's been kidnapped. I need to take a leave of absence."

"*Sonofwarhead*," he swore. "Is she okay? Do you have proof of life? Does Maxine need ransom money?" He rose from his chair, running a hand along his jaw.

Bill knew Claire—had met Claire—when he'd hired the Rider team. Maxine had explained to Mica that Claire had won Bill over by being her usual, exuberant self—showering him with her interest and knowledge in the field of technologically advanced weapons development.

Mica held up a hand in an attempt to stop Bill before he turned one of his few remaining black hairs gray. "I don't know anything yet. I just need time to prepare for whatever's ahead."

"Okay, okay—but let me know if you need anything." He paced his office, his tailored, slate-gray suit catching the sunlight from the office window—shimmering as he moved. "Let me know when she's safe. How's Maxine? Is Maxine okay?"

Probably not, thought Mica. The steely eyed Marine was probably hotter than an M134 minigun firing 3,000 rounds a minute. "The sooner I leave, the sooner I'll have answers."

"Of course, of course—go. Keep me posted."

Mica nodded, turning to leave his office. Five minutes later, she bounded out of the Sharp office building and into her car. On the drive to the Rider SI offices, Mica called her fiancé.

David answered, "Hey, hon. How are you?"

Hearing his calm voice instantly eased her anxiety. Mica had developed her circle of friends around David Rider and his mom, Maxine,—a circle which included Claire Maltisse, Mason Stone, and other Rider employees. Mica would be damned if someone was going to harm any one of her new friends—her soon-to-be family.

Every bone in Mica's body told her that Lucius was behind Claire's disappearance. He was the most dangerous, most ruthless adversary Rider SI had faced since the company's inception. Mica had been familiarizing herself with all of Maxine's relevant files— ever since Maxine had discussed turning the business over to Mica. It wasn't a coincidence that a few months after Rider SI had taken down AJ Schlau, Claire had gone missing.

"I'm okay. I'm heading to Rider headquarters. Claire's missing."

"Missing?" David's pitch rose in alarm.

Mica could hear the bustle of the emergency room through David's phone—beeping monitors, overhead announcements, and the chatter of medical personnel.

"How?"

"Snatched from her house."

"Oh, no! Lucius?"

"He's at the top of my suspect list."

David's voice became distant for a moment—he was telling someone he'd take the radiologist's call in just a minute.

"Anyway," Mica continued. "I called to make sure you're okay. Also, I don't know how long recovering Claire will take—I probably won't be home tonight."

"No worries. Do what you need to do."

"I need you to take care of the security measures I usually do when you get home."

"I'll set the alarm," David assured her.

"And I want the spare gun within your reach at all times."

They'd been together for three months now, but she'd only managed to get him to the gun range once for some basic training. Fortunately, as the son of a Marine, David had paid attention when his mother had taught him about firearms. If he was attacked, he'd be able to defend himself—but the effectiveness of that defense would depend on how many attackers he faced, and how stealthy they were. He was a doctor, not a fighter.

Mica knew she could easily overpower David. She knew how to bypass their home security system—even without the code—and a lone man with basic weapons training and minimal hand-to-hand combat experience posed no great threat to her.

If Mica could take David, anybody on Lucius's payroll could too.

David reassured her, "I'll keep the gun close."

"I love you."

"I love you, too. I expect a call or text when this blows over."

"Will do."

RYAN WALSH THREW the baseball to Reece Owen at the park. Ryan's hands were cold, so the slap of the ball into the leather mitt stung when he caught it—but he'd rather be moving, outside in the chilly air, than sitting in the car doing reconnaissance. Besides, sitting in a car next to the restless, wiry Reece was agony.

"Seriously—these guys are meeting in a park in trench coats and feeding pigeons? Can you get more cliché?" Reece caught the ball Ryan chucked back to him.

Ryan and Reece were a hundred feet away from the men they had under surveillance, and their earpieces let them communicate with each other without having to shout or risk letting eavesdroppers overhear them. Since they'd planted a listening device on the bench itself, right where their targets were ostensibly feeding the pigeons, they could also listen into the conversation of the two men. At the same time, their conversation was also being recorded. The two men were currently discussing business.

"At least we're not stationary," Ryan said.

"I hear that."

At Reece's next throw, Ryan pictured Reece on the pitching mound—his thin, coiled body springing forward as he pitched a fastball just like he'd used to in high school. He and Reece had been inseparable during their high school years—playing baseball together, fishing, and—of course—troublemaking.

After school, they'd joined the Rangers together. The difficulty of their tours of service had provided Ryan and Reece with some of both the best and worst memories of their lives.

After the Rangers, Reece had been driven to drink more than anyone would claim was healthy, while Ryan had been reduced to taking fights for money. Then, along came Maxine Rider—who provided a company and a purpose. Working for her had brought the two men back together and out of their own cycle of self-pity and self-flagellation.

"So, why are these two assholes on Maxine's radar?" Reece asked.

"Didn't you read Max's brief?"

"Of course not. I have you for the short version."

As the men talked in the background, Ryan updated Reece. "Maxine's investigating the guy with the Charlie Chaplin mustache for extortion." From the topic of the discussion on the bench, the men were brokering a deal. "What's puzzling me is that I know the red-bearded man beside him from somewhere. I think if I got a closer look at him, it would trigger the memory."

"Too bad you don't have Mica's photographic memory." Reece caught Ryan's next throw before smoothing down his own mustache—an elegant, fully-realized creation that extended beyond the corners of his lips on either side.

The man who looked like Charlie Chaplin stood from the bench they were observing—shaking hands with Red Beard before walking away. Red Beard took out his phone and either made a call or accepted one—Ryan couldn't tell.

Ryan and Reece had to wait for their second target to abandon the bench before they could retrieve their recording device. They'd heard snippets of the conversation, but Claire would go through the entire dialogue with a fine-tooth comb—teasing out any information with her typical attention to detail; right down to granular details like which breed of pigeon had been cooing in the background.

As he remained on the bench, they listened to Red Beard's conversation.

"Hoyle here," the man said into the phone. "Yeah, I'm done here ... Yes, everything's set up for Maltisse, but I'll check in with the men holding her. I've gotta meet the boss at the club in a few minutes." Finally, he stood and walked away from the bench, still speaking on the phone.

No! No, no!

Ryan and Reece had fallen silent at the mention of Claire's last name—but with the red-bearded Hoyle still on his phone as he walked away from the bench, they wouldn't be able to hear the rest of the one-sided conversation.

"Reece," Ryan hissed, taking off his baseball glove and reaching for his own phone, "I'm going to follow him. You need to..."

"...grab the recorder and get to the car," Reece nodded, as Ryan started following Hoyle. "I'm on it. You keep tailing him."

Ryan kept his distance, phone pressed to his ear as if he was having a phone conversation just like his target was.

Hoyle. Ryan knew that name.

He was one of Lucius Titan's goons—which explained why Ryan had recognized the beard. From Ryan's brief stint working for Lucius, he'd met many unsavory characters. If Hoyle and Lucius were planning something together—something involving Claire—it could only be bad news.

Ryan glanced back at Reece only once—confirming he'd reached the bench to retrieve the recorder. Few things were as sacred as a working partner who could read your mind and improvise when the situation changed.

As he walked, Ryan dialed Maxine.

"Walsh. I'm glad you called." Her gravelly voice was even more gruff than usual.

Ryan's throat constricted.

That didn't sound reassuring.

"Because I'm such a likable guy? Or because you already know something has happened to Claire?"

"She's missing," Max confirmed. "Not at work. Not at home. I just finished checking at her house. Looks like a kidnapping." She paused. "Your turn."

Ryan turned a corner, leaving the park behind and keeping pace with Hoyle.

"We were on the surveillance job you set up. Our mark met up with Hoyle—one of Lucius's employees. We overheard him on a phone call. He said: '*Everything's set up for Maltisse.*' That's all we got before his conversation went out of range. So, they have Claire. Do you know where they've taken her?"

"No."

No—and without Claire's expertise, how could they find her? *Mica.*

Mica was a damn fine tracker. She'd help find Claire.

"Are we assembling?" Ryan asked.

"We are. I've reached out to Mica already. I'll text you a meeting place when I sort it out."

"I'm trailing Hoyle now."

"Snatch him. We need to know what he knows."

"Okay." Ryan looked around as Hoyle took another turn. It'd be hard grabbing a man in broad daylight, right here in downtown Atlanta—but Claire's life could be at risk.

Ryan hung up the phone and called his wife. If Claire had been taken, all of their loved ones might be at risk.

"Hey!" Jenna's cheerful voice answered the phone.

"Hi, hun. How's work?"

"Everything's good here."

Ryan turned the corner—but Hoyle had vanished.

LUCIUS TITAN HUNG up the phone and dropped it into his pocket. He lined up the golf ball with the pin. The sun shone, although a crisp February breeze chilled the air. The pairing of a windbreaker over a collared shirt, worn with a pair of slacks, kept his core warm —while the glove he wore on his left hand protected it from exposure to the cold air.

In a smooth pendulum stroke, Lucius tapped the ball. It rolled six feet across the even surface of Bermuda grass and dropped into the hole.

He was pleased that the putting green had stayed verdant through the winter, even when the rest of the golf course was now bathed in brown. The contrast gave him the sensation of putting on an island of green—an island of money.

Although that metaphor was an accurate one. Given how much money Lucius had paid for his country club membership over the years, he probably *was* rolling his ball across the equivalent of hundreds of dollar bills.

Lucius readjusted his linked fingers, wrapping them snuggly around his putting iron. He smiled at the other man on the green with him. "Thanks to you, we have Claire Maltisse in custody—Maxine Rider's diamond in the rough—and the interrogator is on his way to her soon."

Claire was the computer savvy woman who worked in the background of Rider Security and Investigation. Now, Claire belonged to him.

Hoyle, one of Lucius's newly promoted employees, was the man who'd recently joined him on the green. He was wearing khaki pants and a long-sleeve, collared cotton shirt and a trench coat, which hid his prison tattoos and disguised the hardened criminal's checkered past.

Hoyle listened patiently as Lucius spoke—his thin mouth hidden behind a robust reddish beard. Lucius liked that he was a good listener—not to mention savvy, ruthless, and loyal.

Lucius lined up his putt. "Maxine will be crippled without Claire's computer skills—and when we finish wringing the blue-haired freak of all the business intelligence Rider SI has accumulated, we'll also have access to every one of Maxine's clients' darkest secrets."

Maxine had helped many businesses over the years by

buffering their security. With Claire's knowledge, he could bypass and infiltrate all their systems.

In a smooth pendulum stroke, Lucius tapped the golf ball—watching it roll toward the hole. With a satisfying *clunk*, it dropped inside. Lucius allowed himself to smile, murmuring, "Maxine Rider has interfered too many times in Titan Enterprise's affairs."

"I heard about Russia," Hoyle said.

Maxine had thwarted the Argentinian hit Lucius had helped orchestrate on Russian mobster Vladimir Pronin. After the failed assassination attempt, Maxine had retaliated by launching a Hellfire into a drug production plant outside Aldao. Her actions had threatened to unravel the relationship Lucius had been working to build with Argentinian drug lord Lautaro Fernandez.

But Maxine's egregious meddling had extended beyond just demolishing the cocaine plant, and interfering with his Russian mob hit.

"Did Maxine stop there? No." Lucius lined up another ball on the practice green. "Maxine also stopped our attempted theft of Bill Sharp's drone prototype."

"Then AJ," Hoyle said.

Lucius's grip tightened instinctively, causing him to overshoot the pin by a foot. "Yes," he responded, through gritted teeth. "Then AJ."

Maxine and her team had taken down one of Lucius's top drug dealers—AJ Schlau—although to call him a drug dealer oversimplified his role.

AJ had been upper-level management—in legitimate business terms, his title might have been something like 'President of Supply Chain'. He was responsible for quietly and securely moving shipments of heroin, cocaine, ecstasy, and prostitutes to where they needed to go.

His loss was a large financial setback for Lucius, not to mention it created a difficult-to-fill vacancy in his organization.

Hoyle had some logistics skills, but his strengths made him a better heavy hitter than a people manager. AJ wouldn't be easy to replace. Lucius was hemorrhage money for AJs defense team of lawyers in hopes of getting him aquitted.

All in all, Lucius had underestimated Maxine's little rag-tag team of military misfits—who continued to delude themselves into thinking they stood on some kind of moral high ground.

Every step of the way, ever since Russia, Maxine Rider had been chipping away at Lucius's empire. At first, she'd been no more irritating than a flea. Then, she'd morphed into a tick—stubborn, and harder to eliminate. It wasn't until Maxine had snagged AJ, though— turning him over to the Feds—that Lucius had realized the extent of the risk Maxine now posed to him. She'd evolved into a disease-infested ectoparasite—one that threatened to infect his entire organization.

Lucius Titan had decided then to exterminate her.

He adjusted the glove on his left hand and blew warm air across his exposed right hand, combatting the cool, morning chill.

He didn't look at Hoyle as he spoke. "That former Marine needs to be taught a lesson." Lucius tapped in another putt.

"I could kill her," Hoyle offered calmly.

"We *could* kill her—but a swift death doesn't feel personal enough." Lucius wanted to *gut* Maxine—to rip out and hold her bleeding liver...

Figuratively speaking, of course. He wasn't about to get blood on his Versace suite.

"The best way to bring Rider to her knees is to take her precious hacker—Claire Maltisse—and break her."

Lucius tapped a ball on the green to and fro with the head of his putter. He liked this plan.

Cripple Maxine's business.

Cripple the people she loves.

Cripple Maxine.

3

On the way to pick up Pete from the airport, Drake started making phone calls. He called every Titan employee whose number was stored in his contact list. He pretended he was trying to get a team together for a pick-up game of basketball for the weekend. If they turned him down, he asked them for the number of someone else he knew from the organization, but didn't have contact details for.

The thirteenth person he dialed was someone Drake knew who drove for Chong, one of the Chinese drug dealers who paid Lucius Titan for protection.

"Hello?"

"Hey, it's Drake Rivera." He'd created a fake identity—keeping his real first name—when he'd applied for the private security job with Titan Enterprises. "I'm looking for one more to shoot hoops this weekend. You available?"

"I don't play basketball."

"Okay, no worries. Say, do you have Jeremy's number? I can't find it. I think he plays."

"Sure."

After a few seconds, the man rattled off the number.

"Awesome. Thanks so much."

"Uh, but Jerry ain't available this weekend."

Jerry! Dammit. Drake had said the name wrong.

"Oh, right—the job." Drake snapped his fingers, as if suddenly remembering.

"Yeah, the job. They're going to crack Rider's little blue Smurfette."

Drake's stomach felt suddenly lined with lead. He bit back the urge to vomit. Cracking Claire would involve violence that Drake couldn't stomach. "Well, it's about time." He tried to keep the horror out of his voice.

"Sure is. Too bad you weren't good enough in the sack to also pry her lips open."

"Too bad." Drake hung up the phone before he had to listen to more from the slime ball.

Drake hadn't slept with Claire. They'd kissed, and it had been sizzling enough to make him crave more. But, how could he sleep with her when their relationship had been a sham? He'd planned to tell her the truth—but she'd found out the wrong way, before he'd had a chance to explain.

Even if he got the chance to, Claire would never believe him now—and that was if she even agreed to listen to him.

Drake called Jerry's number. "Jerry, it's Drake. Boss man said I could come watch and learn from the interrogation, but my GPS is all haywire. Can you help me out?"

Drake had no idea who had been put in charge of the operation to kidnap Claire, so he hoped he wouldn't be asked to specify who the 'boss man' he'd referred to actually was. It could be Lucius. It could be Hoyle. In fact, it could be any of a dozen lackeys who answered to Hoyle.

Apparently, though, the deception worked.

Drake heard Jerry dragging on a cigarette. "This shithole's in the middle of nowhere. So, after you get off the highway, take a left from Old Highway Five onto 382. Then, right on Flat Creek School Road…"

Drake listened through the Blue Tooth speakers as he jotted a few quick notes down on the nearest scrap of paper—a script he'd been practicing for an upcoming radio commercial. When Jerry finished giving directions, Drake thanked him and hung up.

Drake pulled into the parking lane at the airport marked Arrivals. The dense traffic was giving Drake anxious palpitations. He should have told Pete to take a ride share and meet him somewhere later—so he could get to the cabin and find Claire faster. But he already felt like a jerk for forgetting Pete's flight—and he needed his friend's help.

Pete appeared at the doorway and crossed the sidewalk to Drake's car. He hoisted his suitcase into the backseat and climbed into the passenger seat—remarking: "Are you aware there's a beast in the back of your car?"

"He's Claire's dog."

"They killed her dog?"

"He's alive."

"So, you kidnapped her dog?"

"If I show up with Bear, it might be the only thing that keeps Claire from killing me."

Bear was like Claire's child. Right now, she was probably more worried about Bear's safety than her own. Bringing Bear with him not only kept the dog safe, but would also give Claire immediate peace of mind when she saw her furry baby alive and well.

"What if he wakes up?" Pete asked.

"Let's hope we've got Claire back by that time."

"Okay—so, what are you doing to get her back?"

Drake regarded his scrawny friend, sitting there with his full head of bushy, dark curls. He and Peter had been friends since grade school, yet couldn't be more different. Pete lived a sedentary life in front of a computer screen—literally playing games with commentary for money—while Drake was an extrovert who'd made a modest career for himself in Hollywood. Yet, the two of them could relax in each other's company and have a good time talking and joking effortlessly.

As he checked the mirrors, Drake outlined his plan. "I'm going to distract this guy Jerry, and whoever else is with him, while Claire escapes."

"How are you going to distract a criminal?"

Drake scoffed. "I'm an actor, Pete—distraction and deception are what I do." Drake pulled his Explorer away from the curb, leaving the airport behind.

"Ohh-kay," Pete asked, "and if that doesn't work?"

"Then, instead of staged fighting, I'll be doing the real thing. I've got Claire's Taser." He glanced at Pete, who always wore the same multi-pocket jacket. "Let me borrow your jacket."

Pete ran his hands down his chest, his lower lip protruding. "This is my favorite jacket."

"I know."

"It has seventeen pockets."

"I know."

Pete inserted his hands into two of the pockets at the sides. "I have *stuff* in these pockets."

"Leave your stuff—I only need one pocket to hold the Taser. I'll give it back as soon as I'm done."

CLAIRE ROTATED her neck in slow circles. Every part of her felt stiff and sore. How long had she been tied to this chair?

She looked around at the cabin walls. She was being held in a bedroom, though the only furniture was the chair that she was bound to. One wall had a window, one wall a closet, one wall the door, and the fourth wall—her stomach lurched—had shackles dangling from it.

Keep it together, Claire.

What would her boss—and a former Marine—do in this situation?

How would Maxine Rider approach this?

Claire knew that Max would first look for an escape. No— she'd *first* look for a weapon. Claire's eyes darted to the menacing wall opposite. The shackles hanging there looked heavy enough to crack a skull—but they were bolted to the wall.

Claire looked around again. Maybe she could find a loose floorboard.

She looked down at the hardwood floor. The warped planks were covered with blood stains and bleach stains—as though someone had tried to scrub the floor clean, but when they'd real- ized they were stripping the floorboards and couldn't remove all the blood stains, they threw bleach over it and gave up.

The door rattled.

Claire looked up as two men entered the room. Claire recog- nized them as goons who worked for Lucius Titan. She kept files on every one of Lucius's employees—well, the ones she knew about, anyway—and these two were familiar.

Claire didn't have the names and faces of all of Titan's associates memorized—but she'd definitely seen these men's profiles before. They were lower tier henchmen, but nevertheless military-trained and unquestionably lethal.

Like the computers she was so adept with, Claire's brain

started computing. Judging by the age of these two men, they couldn't have served in the military for more than ten years.

One of the men had a crew cut, and the other wore a ponytail. Since they weren't hiding their identity with masks, Claire suspected that nobody intended her to live through this kidnapping.

She took a deep breath.

What would Max do?

Claire summed up the courage of her boss, and greeted the two new arrivals with a glared, narrow-eyed expression. "Cozy cabin you've got here." She tried to keep her voice hard and frosty, so as not to betray the fear zinging through her nerves like a pinball in an arcade game.

The man with the ponytail stood in front of Claire and put his hands on his hips. He growled, "Benny and I want to offer you a choice. You share all of Maxine Rider's secrets with *us*—" he motioned a hand between the two of them "—and you'll never have to meet the *real* interrogator." Then, he leaned closer. "I've seen that guy's work. He'll turn your pretty face and that tight little body into a bloody Picasto by the time he's finished."

"It's *Picasso*," the guy with the crew cut, Benny, corrected his partner.

Claire looked between the two of them, gauging their level of intelligence. These two looked like the snatch-and-grab muscle—and she suspected they weren't the brightest of the bunch. Still, she needed to proceed cautiously—to bide her time, but not piss them off.

"You work for Lucius?" she asked.

"The *who* isn't as important as the *why*," said the guy with the ponytail—Picasso.

"What's the why?"

"Like I said," Picasso growled, "we want information on Maxine Rider."

"What kind of information?"

"Clients. Hideouts. *Inside* information."

"Bill Sharp." Claire offered. Lucius already knew about the weapons manufacturer, so she wasn't divulging any classified information.

Picasso licked his lips. "Yeah, good start. Why don't you tell us about *him*?"

"Nice guy," Claire started. "Genius, really. About six feet tall, graying hair—full head of hair, too, which is admirable at his age..."

Picasso lunged at Claire, causing her to recoil back—but he stopped short of actually touching her. "Don't get cute."

Claire had her back pressed against the chair—as far away from Picasso as the bindings around her ankles and wrists would let her go. She swallowed dryly and shook her head, eyes wide. "Sorry. I talk a lot sometimes when I'm nervous."

Picasso kept himself within Claire's personal space. The scent of cigarettes wafted off him toward her. She looked at his yellow-stained teeth and flat, broad nose.

"So, talk," Picasso demanded, "but keep it relevant. Tell us about his high-tech weapons."

Claire gave several bobs of her head as she eyed the two men warily. The large men intimidated her, though they weren't nearly as slick as the Rider men.

What to tell them—and how to buy time?

Claire took a deep breath before launching into a fictional account of Bill Sharp.

"Well, he's got tech like no military has seen. Like those dilithium crystals that power a positron cortex. Wicked cool."

"What does it do?"

"It's classified."

Picasso shot Claire a warning look.

"Okay. Okay." Her imagination raced. "It's an artificial intelligence designed to power a fleet of drones. Human soldiers will be a thing of the past." An idea struck her: "Imagine an army of transformers."

"Like the movie?"

She lowered her voice and held Picasso's gaze. "*Better* than the movie."

Picasso, evidently under the impression Claire was sharing valuable information, leaned back and began taking notes on his phone. "How do you spell that? The crystals?"

"Di-lith-ium," Claire enunciated.

Eagerly, he entered it into his phone. "And they power what?"

"Positron Cortex."

"Where's it stored?" Picasso demanded.

"Mr. Sharp has a secret lab, deep beneath Stone Mountain. It cost a billion dollars just to build the place."

Picasso looked up, his eyes widening. "Like Batman?"

"Exactly," Claire nodded. Her tone of voice was conspiratorial —as if she were proud he'd made that connection. In reality, though, her tone indicated the delight she felt in him falling for her nonsense. Picasso was oblivious—taking her tone as a compliment about his nuanced understanding of complex weapons.

"What else?" he demanded.

Claire shook her head. "I've already said too much—I could lose my job."

Ha! That part was laughable. Maxine would never fire Claire— but Claire hoped these men could relate to the fear of losing their job, especially given the ruthless reputation of Lucius Titan.

Benny, who'd been silently listening, stepped forward and painfully grabbed a fistful of Claire's blue hair. She winced, tears springing to her eyes.

"In case we didn't make it clear, lady," the henchman growled, "your *life* is on the line—forget your *job*."

Claire let out a whimper as her hair was stretched from her scalp.

"Okay, okay," she gasped. "The real *pièce de résistance* is the flux capacitor."

She exhaled gratefully when Benny released her, shaking her head and taking a steadying breath. Her fear was real, even if her words weren't. "The flux capacitor, though—it's unstable. Transporting it—say, like if you were stealing it—would be highly risky. In fact, you'd have to know how to reverse the polarity."

Picasso listened with rapt intensity. "Can *you* do that?"

"*I* can—but you'd have to create the right spacio-temporal hyperlink. I'd need the t-1000 for that."

"What's the t-1000?"

"Sky Net prototype. It uses tachyons combined with midichlorians."

"Midichlorians?" Something like recognition flickered in Picasso's eyes.

Son of a hicismus, Claire silently swore. She held her breath. Maybe the Star Wars reference had been pushing it too far with these buffoons. Soon, they might realize she was feeding them technobabble bullshit from her favorite shows and movies.

Nevertheless, Claire kept a straight face—or rather, fear kept her face straight.

"They're elementary particles." Claire looked back and forth between Benny and Picasso. "Never heard of them? It's okay— most people haven't." She took a deep breath and continued: "Anyway, the point is that reversing the polarity is tricky, but it *can* be done—if you have someone with skills. If you mess it up, though, even your dog tags wouldn't survive the subsequent incineration." Claire gave a nervous chuckle. "But, '*the spice must flow.*' Am I right?"

Picasso furrowed his brow and nodded. Benny gave her a

puzzled look—like he was starting to suspect she'd been taking some of Titan's illegal drugs.

Claire squeezed her eyes shut for one, long moment.

Had these guys never seen the movie *Dune*? Maybe *this* was the brilliant torture technique Titan had planned for her—to simply stick her in a room with two men who understood none of her science fiction and pop culture references.

Claire might have gone mad—if it hadn't been working so well to her advantage.

She looked desperately between the two men. "Listen. In the end, life is a choice—red pill, or blue?"

Picasso stood and looked at Benny, who gave him a confused shrug in return—as if Claire was either brilliant, or crazy.

They started to walk toward the door.

"Hey—word of caution, guys," Claire called after them.

They turned to look back at her.

"Don't cross the streams."

Picasso looked first at his crotch, then at Benny's. "Is that some type of perverted joke?"

Claire dropped her chin to her chest. She'd been making a *Ghostbusters* reference, and they'd thought she was talking about urinating.

"No," Claire deadpanned. "If you plan on high jacking a shipment from Sharp, you simply need to be careful with the equipment—especially the proton packs."

"What do they do?"

"Used correctly, they can incinerate living flesh from behind six feet of solid rock wall. Used incorrectly..." She shook her head. "Protoplasmic, apocalyptic-level destruction."

She hoped they didn't ask what *protoplasmic, apocalyptic-level destruction* meant—because she had no idea.

Benny and Picasso exchanged confused glances, and then they left the room, closing the door behind them.

Claire relaxed slightly—but she knew these stalling tactics could only be dragged out for so long. Time was already running out.

DRAKE AND PETE left Atlanta behind them as they headed north.

As Drake drove to the remote cabin Jerry had given him the address of—the one clandestinely owned by Titan Enterprise—he consciously tried not to drive so fast that he'd attract the attention of the Georgia State Troopers. Nevertheless, his foot bore the weight of the worry gnawing at his insides. Was Claire being tortured even now?

Using the Bluetooth in his Explorer, he dialed Maxine Rider's number. As CEO of the company, she had a listed mobile phone number.

Drake glanced at Pete. "This isn't going to be pretty, so brace yourself—and keep quiet."

The woman's voice answering the phone sounded thick and gravelly. "Rider Security and Investigation."

"Maxine Rider?"

"This is she." Maxine Rider had no southern charm, no northern twang, and no Midwest accent. Her voice was flat and strictly business.

"My name is Drake Fitzgerald, and I know where Claire is."

There was a pause, before finally: "She's safe?"

"She's not."

That flat, strictly business voice suddenly turned sharp and dead. "You've got ten seconds to tell me where she is, before I find you and cut off your..."

Drake grimaced as Maxine unleashed five seconds of verbal fury at him—so loud that the speakers of his Explorer crackled. Pete's jaw dropped open as he listened, but he kept quiet.

Eventually, when Maxine gave Drake the opportunity to speak, he explained, "Lucius's men took her. I'll give you directions. Do you have something to write on?"

"Start talking," she barked.

Drake gave her directions to the cabin.

"How do you know this?" Maxine asked.

"I used to work for Titan."

Another pause.

"I don't understand—Claire said you were an actor."

"I am."

Maxine gave in irritated grunt. "How is it you're an actor *and* you used to work for Titan?"

"I faked a military resume and took a job with Titan to get undercover experience." He sighed. "I thought it would improve my acting."

She gave an audible scoff. "Where are you now?"

"I'm heading to the cabin."

"You and what army?"

Drake glanced at Pete. "Just me."

"Bullshit. You stay put until my team catches up with you, and *we'll* orchestrate the rescue."

"There isn't time. I don't know what they're doing to her even now." Drake gripped the wheel tighter. His palms began to sweat.

"You're an actor." Maxine's voice was cold. "Titan's men are former military—trained in weapons and hand-to-hand combat." She snorted. "*They* won't be acting—and they won't be using fake guns, blunted and retracting knives, or firing blanks."

"I know that." Drake tried to keep the irritation out of his voice.

Maxine sounded just as irritated—if not more so. "You go in there and screw this up, you could put Claire in more danger than she already is."

"I'm *not* waiting. I've got the element of surprise."

"*My* team will do the extraction."

"I'll call you when she's safe," Drake said with finality.

The call disconnected.

Pete glanced over at him, eyebrows raised. "That is one pissed off Mama Hen."

Drake rolled his shoulders as he took the exit ramp off the interstate. "Well, I guess if Lucius's men don't kill me, Maxine Rider will."

4

———

*M*axine tapped at her steering wheel with quick, stabbing motions as she drove north. She shot a brief glare at her phone in the dash holder, where it rested silently after she'd hung up on Drake.

Drake.

Claire's boyfriend—or whatever he was—had sounded genuinely worried about Claire, but Maxine didn't like the idea of an amateur attempting a rescue.

She zipped her car past bare spruce and oaks. Tall pines speared the pale, gray horizon. She'd be planting her garden soon—another month.

Maxine instructed her phone to call Ryan Walsh.

"Max—any news?"

"Walsh, I need you and Reece en route north now. I'll text the directions. For now, just get on Highway 19, northbound."

"We're on the move. What's the update on Claire?"

Maxine loved that her employees were unwavering in their trust, loyalty, and willingness to act. She heard the shuffling of feet and suspected Reece and Ryan were already making haste to their vehicle.

"I have an address now—her location. We'll rendezvous at the gas station off the highway—you, Reece, me, and maybe Mica, if she can make it." From where Mica would be coming from, she might get bogged down in by the Atlanta traffic.

"I'm glad you know where she is, but could this be some type of trap?"

"Claire's boyfriend called me after I discovered her missing."

"Claire has a boyfriend?"

"Well, someone she's seen a few times. Anyway, this guy—Drake Fitzgerald—tells me he used to work for Titan."

"This guy put Claire in danger?" Ryan growled.

"If I'm honest, Walsh—I'm the one who put her in danger. My quarrel with Lucius has been a boiling cauldron that finally spilled over. I should have taken more precautions to protect Claire. Fitzy was just a tool for Titan—one that didn't work out so well, since he's on Claire's side now."

Maxine had taken safety measures. Claire's house, her Jeep, and the Rider offices all had security systems in place—but those were merely deterrents against average criminals. Lucius Titan was anything but average. If he'd wanted to get past Maxine's home or office security, he had the funds and brainpower at his disposal to do it.

Maxine heard Ryan switch her to speakerphone—probably the Bluetooth in his car—and she heard him update Reece before talking to her again.

"Maxine—we've got two handguns, four clips, one shotgun, and some tear gas. What's the plan?"

Without Claire on reconnaissance, or someone readily available to do her job, Maxine couldn't know the schematics of the house Claire was being held at, in order to formulate an organized attack. "We're going to have to make an onsite determination once we know all entry and exit points."

"How many hostiles?"

With time and planning, Maxine could have used a drone to canvas the place—maybe even one capable of reading heat signatures and telling her how many jarheads they were up against.

Time, however, was a luxury none of them had to enjoy.

"I don't know." Maxine felt the road rumbling beneath her speeding tires, but she felt as if she was traveling at a snail's pace. "Fitzy's on his way there now."

"Can he do recon? What's his background?"

Maxine coughed. Ryan was making the logical assumption that Drake Fitzgerald would have had military background if he'd worked for Titan.

"He can't recon." She took a deep breath. "He's an actor."

"An actor?" Reece's voice sounded incredulous through the speakerphone.

"I'm confused," Ryan said.

"As you should be," Maxine agreed. "Fitzy took a job with Titan to improve his acting. He wanted experience to see what it would be like working for a private security company."

"He wanted it for *acting* purposes? And Titan's HR department didn't catch that?" Ryan's voice now matched Reece's level of incredulity.

"Maybe they didn't—or maybe they did, and Lucius decided to use him anyway. I don't know."

"But—he's an *actor*? He was working in order to research a role?"

"For authenticity, I suppose. It's not unheard of—Robert DeNiro drove a cab around New York even as he was filming *Taxi Driver*. Method acting, I think they call it."

"Huh," Ryan scoffed. "I guess I remember hearing that Daniel Day-Lewis spent six months in the wild trapping and skinning animals before filming *The Last of the Mohicans*."

"Ed Harris built a painting studio and learned to paint for *Pollock*," Maxine added.

"I didn't see that one."

Reece cleared his throat, interjecting: "So this actor—Fitzy—is our link to finding Claire?"

"Yeah," Maxine said. "Except he isn't waiting for us."

"What?" Ryan and Reece said in unison.

"He's afraid the interrogation is eminent—so he's determined to go in now."

This time, Reece lit up the phone with cursing. "Some *civilian* is going to make a half-assed rescue attempt? He'll get Claire killed!"

"I don't like it either, Reece. You want to bitch about it? Or help me come up with a productive plan?" Maxine agreed with his sentiments, but she needed focused soldiers—not emotionally distracted hotheads.

When Maxine hung up the phone with Ryan and Reece, she pulled into a gas station to fuel up her Crossover. When the tank was full, she shook off the chill from standing outside and climbed back into her car—phoning Mason via Face Time.

His blonde hair and blue eyes came briefly into view before the camera lens of his phone pointed towards a brick wall and a cobblestone walkway. "One sec, Max."

Maxine heard heavy breathing followed by masculine grunting. The familiar crunch of fist meeting flesh preceded the shuffling of boots on screen. Those boots vanished quickly—replaced by the sight of a man landing face down on the cobblestone. His pockmarked cheek was squished against the ground as Mason pressed a knee into his back.

Mason was currently stationed in New Orleans on a missing person's case, which meant this fight was probably taking place somewhere near Bourbon Street. The man beneath Mason's knee grimaced, and Maxine wondered if it was from the stench of the human secretions on the street as much as from the pain of being restrained.

Mason bent down and pulled his captive's hands behind his back, securing them with a twist tie. He rolled the man on his back. "Stay," he said firmly.

Mason picked up the phone and came into full view again. "Hey, Max. What's up?" His casual tone sounded as if he was at a picnic flipping burgers on the grill, rather than pummeling a man into submission.

"Is that gentleman the key to your missing person's case?"

"I don't know yet. He didn't cooperate with friendly conversation, so we need to have a more forceful questioning."

The methodology of various Rider team members wasn't always strictly legal, but time was critical in an abduction—and Maxine had authorized her men and women to use force when absolutely necessary for theirs or their client's sake.

"We've got a situation here. Claire is missing. Lucius is behind it. Ryan, Reece, Mica, and I are assembling now."

"You need me back?" Mason's eyes clouded with worry.

"Not yet. Maybe soon, if things get worse."

"What's worse than Claire being missing? No. You know what? Don't answer that."

"The main thing I need you to do is try to wrap up your case, get back here as soon as you can, and watch your six. I don't know if Lucius is targeting only Claire, or if he has his sights set bigger."

"No problem. You'll keep me posted?"

"As soon as I know more, you'll know more."

On Maxine's screen, a text from Vladimir popped into view: *Red or white wine tonight?*

She ignored the message. She didn't have time to think about wine.

"Mason, I need to get back on the road. I'll message you later."

DRAKE REMEMBERED the first time he'd met Claire. He'd staged the event—his knight in shining armor scheme had been straight out of a Humphrey Bogart movie.

After Titan Enterprises had hired him, Drake had done security chauffeur work for a month. It had been excessively boring—nothing like the action and suspense of the movies. His work had been more *Driving Miss Daisy*—minus the witty banter—than *The Transporter*.

Then, Drake had been assigned to Claire. His mission had been to get close to her—to learn her patterns and find any weaknesses in her routine or security. He'd been told she'd attempted to compromise Titan's missions and clients. Drake had researched the role as if he was playing a part in a Steven Spielberg movie.

For a solid week, he'd watched Claire park in the garage and take the elevators up to the Rider offices. The first time he'd seen her—mid-twenties, with a vibrant blue bob cut—he'd thought: How could this woman be a threat to anyone?

Did anyone even take her seriously?

To answer those questions, he'd asked around at Titan Enterprises. Apparently, Claire worked for the rival security company to Titan Enterprises—Rider Security and Investigation.

Rider SI had been trying to sabotage Titan Enterprises for several years, and this blue-haired woman supposedly possessed crazy computer skills. She'd been trying to break into Titan's systems.

Corporate espionage. Drake thought he could play a role in order to find information to bolster Titan's digital defense. He hadn't known at the time that Titan Enterprises was the company with all the dirty secrets.

So, Drake had watched Claire, all the while thinking himself terribly clever. Her work hours were unpredictable. Although she arrived at the offices of Rider SI every day between seven and eight, she left at varying times—from any time in the early afternoon to late into the evenings.

She took the occasional Friday off, and also worked random weekends about once a month. When Claire wasn't working, she took her dog—her *enormous* dog, with a jaw wide enough to clamp fully around a grown man's neck—to the local dog parks and on walks along the Atlanta BeltLine.

After Drake had felt his reconnaissance was sufficient, he'd made his move. He'd detached the positive cable from her Jeep battery and laid in wait—hiding a few cars down in the parking garage.

At the end of her workday, Claire had approached her car. She'd worn a purple, pleated skirt, black tights, and a white blouse. After she climbed into her Jeep, the vehicle unsurprisingly failed to start. Claire popped the hood and stared at the engine before calmly withdrawing her phone.

That was when Drake emerged from between the cars, straightening his suit and pretending to stumble across Claire's predicament serendipitously.

"Need a hand?"

Without looking up at him, she replied, "I don't think so."

Claire typed on her phone with her thumbs at a dizzying speed. Then, she held her phone under the hood of her Jeep to take a picture. That had been followed by more expert thumb typing.

Drake leaned in to look at the engine. "Looks like..."

"...the red battery cable is loose." Claire pocketed her phone and retrieved some type of multipurpose tool from her glove compartment.

"I..." That was the moment she glanced up at Drake, as if noticing him as a human being for the first time. For a moment, she stumbled over her words, looking flushed. "I've got this."

Drake grinned. It was obvious that Claire found him attractive—so, he'd made one step in the right direction already.

Claire tucked a strand of blue hair behind her ear before reattaching the red cable. She tightened the attachment with her multipurpose tool.

Well, so much for the damsel in distress. Maybe he should have faked his own car trouble, and then Claire could have rescued *him*.

"I'm Drake." While he hadn't fixed her car, Drake still had his charm and his looks to work with. On a Hollywood scale, he was average—a solid 5 out of 10. Maybe he could push it to a 7 with the right smoldering pose.

But for the standards of downtown Atlanta—in a parking garage, mid-afternoon—he was definitely a 10 out of 10. He smiled and extended a hand, which Claire left pointedly unshaken.

"Thanks for *offering* to help."

Not "thanks for helping"—because she helped herself.

Claire climbed into her Jeep, started the engine, and pulled forward so quickly that Drake was forced to jump back out of her way.

He'd watched her drive away from him. Baffled, he pulled his phone out of his pocket as he walked back to his Explorer.

It rang twice before being answered.

"Pete? How are you?"

"Good, man. Wrapping up work. How was the big day?"

"It fizzled."

"Ouch. A woman who didn't fall for the Fitzgerald charm? Welcome to the world of us ordinary folk."

"But I have the winning smile!"

"I told you it wouldn't work—not in a parking garage. No woman wants to be alone in a parking garage with a stranger, even if he's wearing Clive Christian cologne and a suit."

"But—I flashed the smile!"

Disheartened, Drake climbed into his car.

"No sketchy villain has this set of teeth like these." Three years of agonizing braces as a teenager, plus monthly whitening treatments, had given Drake a million-dollar smile. Woman typically swooned over his smile—but all it had earned from Claire was a blush and a goodbye. No, not even a goodbye.

"I've gotta come up with Plan B." Drake ran a hand through his hair before starting the engine of his car. Claire had given him a dose of humility that felt sobering—but, at the same time, also presented a challenge. Drake liked challenges.

"You'd better get creative," Pete warned, "because it'll be creepy if you pop-up all of a sudden again."

"I know."

"She's got a dog, right?"

***

CLAIRE SAT in the hard chair in that cabin bedroom, trying not to think about the torture and dismemberment that potentially awaited her.

What were her kidnappers waiting for? Was forcing her to sit in this hard, uncomfortable chair part of their evil plan? Were they softening her up for more interrogation?

Claire thought about Drake again, and how deceptive he'd been. She remembered the first time she'd met Drake. The sun had shone on a bright, Saturday afternoon in Atlanta. Claire had been walking Bear along the BeltLine. The big dog calmly observed the other pedestrians and pets, but took no interest in making anyone's acquaintance. His loyalty belonged exclusively to Claire. Bear liked everyone he'd met from the Rider team, but unless Claire made an effort to introduce her Bullmastiff to other people, Bear didn't seek attention.

Then, a man in blue jeans and a gray T-shirt had approached from the opposite direction. He was walking a boisterous Jack Russell Terrier—or, perhaps the dog was walking *him*. The animal strained to run against the harness.

The Jack Russell was mostly white, with splashes of caramel on his feet and face. As soon as he spotted him, the little dog made a beeline for Bear—barking sharply.

"Heel, Blitz!" The man called a useless command at the yapping terrier—with no true authority or conviction to his tone. Unsurprisingly, the little dog ignored him.

Bear didn't flinched when the little dog bounded right up to him and barked loudly in his face. Instead, Bear emitted a low, growling rumble—instantly causing the Jack Russell to freeze, ears plastered back against his head and his eyes wide.

"Wow, maybe your dog should train Blitz."

Claire regarded the terrier's owner—recognizing the smile, but unable to place where she'd seen it before. She felt no warning alarms—this stranger wasn't anyone on Maxine's watch list.

"Have we met?"

"Yeah, I think we have." The handsome man narrowed his eyes. "You're the woman with the battery problem, right?"

"Ah—the parking garage." Claire remembered.

"I'm Drake." He extended his hand.

Claire shook it, noting Bear's uncharacteristically stiff posture toward Drake.

The man seemed friendly enough, and he was handsome—

with long, sandy blond hair, a dazzling smile, and a deep California tan. He was probably five to seven years older than Claire—but Claire was more interested in what Bear sensed about him.

Nothing outwardly hostile, or her Bullmastiff would have put himself between her and this handsome stranger—but nevertheless, it was clear that Bear didn't trust him.

"Claire." She introduced herself.

"Claire." Drake smiled again, this time as if he'd won something—like meeting her was a delightful treat.

Blitz began tugging at the leash, ready to move on to the next set of sights and smells.

Claire looked at the forceful little dog and laughed. "You need obedience training."

"Do I? We've only just met." Drake wriggled his eyebrows at her.

Claire chuckled as she felt her cheeks redden at Drake's flirtation, and then gestured down at the terrier.

"Oh, I get it," Drake laughed. "You mean Blitz."

"No. I really meant you," Claire fired back. "You need to learn how to help your dog be obedient."

"Well, he's not actually mine. I'm walking him for a friend. I love dogs, but I travel too much to have one of my own." Drake then begun to extend a hand toward Bear. "Who's your friend?"

"No petting," Claire quickly warned him. "Bear has to develop friendships on his own terms."

Drake's hand froze, a foot from Bear's muzzle. "Bear. Well, I suppose it's a suitable name."

They'd walked the next mile of the BeltLine together, and Claire had learned that Drake was an actor—mostly a stunt double, with some small movie parts and some commercial voiceovers on his resume. She'd learned they shared a love for Chinese food and hiking. Claire had suggested certain trails in Georgia he should try while he was visiting the state, and he'd asked her out for dinner in response.

The door of the room rattled.

Claire was yanked from her reminiscence as Benny and Picasso burst into the room, red-faced and fuming—like a couple of hot-tempered Klingons.

Gigs up, she cringed. *They've shared notes with a sci-fi fan.*

5

———

When Picasso lashed out his hand, Claire jumped—but she was restrained by the ties binding her wrists to the chair. Instead of the violent blow she'd expected, though, a phone was held directly in front of her instead.

Claire looked at the face staring back at her.

Hoyle.

Hoyle was goon who worked for Lucius. Claire recognized him from her files. He'd taken the place of AJ Schlau in Lucius's operation, after AJ had been arrested.

Hoyle had a thick, red Viking beard and stared out of the screen with a pair of pale, gray eyes—as cold as if he'd stared down an iceberg and stolen its frigid, unyielding essence.

Picasso let out a low growl. "Boss man says you played us, lady.

Says you was quoting mumbo-jumbo from movies. He counted at least six movies you referenced—and says nothing you told us was legit."

Claire gave Hoyle a hesitant smile. "At last, I meet someone from Lucius's team who's cultured. What was the big give away? The *Back to the Future* flux capacitor? The T-1000 *Terminator* reference?"

Hoyle's lips quirked, but his grey eyes remained flat—dead and cold, like an arctic winter.

"Miss Maltisse, we'll extract the information we want from you —willingly or unwillingly."

"Hey, if you're unwilling, we can skip the interrogation all together," Claire quipped. "I'm not here to inconvenience anyone."

"Whether *you're* willing or unwilling," Hoyle clarified.

"Oh, right." She sighed.

"The interrogator for *unwilling* participants will arrive soon— so, you only have a brief window of opportunity to cooperate with us and spare yourself the agony."

Claire tried to control the shaking in her legs. She masked it by bouncing one leg rapidly on the floor—strumming her fingers on the armrest of the chair, where her hands were tied, as if she was hammering out a drum solo.

As she sat there, her mind raced: *What would Max do?*

Hoyle continued: "I know what you're thinking. You want to stall and give yourself time to be rescued—but no one even knows where you are, Miss Maltisse. Your friends are clueless."

Ha! If only you knew, she thought.

Hoyle added: "You might also be hesitant because we've made no effort to conceal our faces—so, you're probably asking yourself: What's the point of divulging sensitive information if you're a dead woman anyway?"

Claire stilled, confirming his assumption.

Hoyle explained: "The answer is because there are worse things than death, Miss Maltisse. *Much* worse things."

Claire's mind flashed to the movie *Goonies*—specifically the scene during which a young, terrified Chunk was going to have his hand pressed into a churning blender if he didn't divulge the whereabouts of his friends.

Next, she thought about the awful torture scene in *Casino Royale*, and then the skin peeling in *Red Sparrow*. Feeling suddenly flushed and dizzy, Claire wished for the first time in her life that she hadn't seen so many movies—many of which now bombarded her imagination with torture scenes.

"Okay, okay."

Hoyle's bland look suggested he remained unconvinced—but he nevertheless ordered: "Jerry—disconnect this call and record her confession. Send me the voice file, and I'll confirm it."

When Jerry—who was shockingly not *actually* named Picasso—did as instructed, Claire began her babbling.

She spoke rapidly and anxiously, as anybody facing torture and death might be likely to do. This time, she also avoided any mainstream culture movie references—but that didn't make her confession any more real. Instead, she rattled on about weapons programs that didn't exist, and technology that was largely imaginary.

Staying sharp during this fictional information dump at least kept Claire's mind off the terrifying prospect of torture, pain, debilitation, and death.

But that prospect remained. Hoyle was right when he'd claimed that Maxine wouldn't know where Claire was being held—and even if she'd stormed into Lucius's office with an AK-47 and all of the Rider team to back her up, Max would never make it to Claire before the *real* interrogator arrived at the cabin.

One way or another, Lucius's men would get *factual* information out of Claire soon enough—probably only as long as it took her to be confronted with a sharp object, or anything connected to a power supply.

MICA PARKED in the parking deck of the Rider SI building and rushed up to the offices, pressing key codes along the way. She reached the weapons room and began filling a duffel bag with everything the team would need.

As she worked, Mica battled to keep fear from slowing her down, or causing her to make mistakes. She couldn't stop imagining what horrible things Claire was enduring at that moment, even as Mica checked clips and carefully packaged grenades.

Grenades? She paused for a second. Were they overkill?

No.

Mica planned to bring an arsenal sufficient for a small army.

It might *take* an army to rescue Claire. Poor, poor Claire—who was the most vulnerable of them all. Would they break her before the Rider team could reach her?

As Mica packed the bag, secured the weapons, and made her way back to her car, she thought of the time she and Claire had gone to play LASER tag.

Claire had looked futuristic—clad in black spandex, with her white headband and blue hair bright in the ultraviolet light. She'd been carrying a glowing, automatic battle rifle; looking every bit the space-age heroine.

During the game, Mica had tried to teach Claire evasive moves like tumbling and covert techniques like stealth—teaching real combat moves even as they played a harmless game of LASER tag together.

However, the time had overall been spent more on play than real-world practice; and in light of Claire's kidnapping, Mica now wished she'd taken her friend to weekly training sessions at a real facility, rather than time spent at the arcade together. She'd taken Claire to the gun range once last month—but how much could rifle practice prepare anyone for being kidnapped?

Within minutes, Mica was back on the road—roaring up the interstate heading north. She maneuvered deftly around Atlanta traffic, with her speed ranging from sixty to seventy miles per hour. Even at that breakneck speed, though, the journey still felt agonizingly slow under the circumstances.

A LITTLE FURTHER NORTH, Ryan stared out the window as Reece drove.

"We'll get her back, man," Reece promised.

Ryan nodded—but would they really?

Ryan knew from experience what Lucius was capable of. He'd already witnessed the ruthless man's lack of hesitation in maiming and killing people.

To distract himself, he murmured, "You remember the first time we met Claire?"

"Yeah," Reece snorted. "She stared up at you like you were larger than life—and then poked a finger into your bicep to see if it would deflate."

Ryan chuckled. Claire had always been like a younger, giddy sister to him, ever since their first encounter. She'd been excited he'd taken the job to work for Maxine, citing the detailed vetting of his background that Claire had personally undertaken.

The amount of information she'd unearthed about Ryan had been disconcerting—but had also spoken to how valuable somebody with her unique skills could be.

"The first time we did a job with her on coms, I was crackin' up," Reece added his own reminisces. "There we were, taking gunfire, and she's cheerfully making movie references about *Iron Man*."

"She's cool under pressure," Ryan nodded.

"Yeah, well—she wasn't the one gettin' shot at."

"Still, she knew we were in danger, and she re-routed us to safety."

Claire had kept her calm and her wits—working surefootedly under pressure to ensure the safety of her friends and colleagues. It had been the first of many.

But being kidnapped was a whole different level of intensity—and Ryan didn't want to think about how terrified Claire must be, chained in a basement somewhere.

Claire would know the purpose of the kidnapping, too—which would make it all the more terrifying for her. This wasn't about ransom. Lucius didn't need Maxine's money. This was about information. Claire probably had a terabyte of data on Rider SI memorized, which was exactly what Lucius wanted to hack. Maxine had made an effort to keep Claire off Lucius's radar, but he'd apparently discerned Claire's role anyway; and now her life was on the line as a result.

"Mica's gotta be pissed," Reece said. He was as aware as anybody how close Mica and Claire had become in the few short months they'd known each other.

Ryan turned his gaze from the road ahead to Reece. "If anything happens to Claire, Lucius will get the full wrath of Rider SI."

—⚓—

CLAIRE WATCHED with apprehension as Jerry and Benny came back into the room she was imprisoned in. She suspected they'd sent the voice file to Hoyle and were now waiting for him to research her confession. Yet, something had changed in Jerry's bland expression. His eyes had sharpened and there was a menacing new swagger to his steps.

Jerry approached Claire, taking a long swig from a water bottle. Judging by the condensation, the liquid was cool. Jerry then unleashed a melodramatic, satisfied sigh. He tilted the bottle toward her.

"Care to wet your whistle?"

Claire felt thirsty enough not to care about drinking after this vile man. She nodded, craning her neck toward the water bottle.

Snickering, Jerry pulled it away before a drop spilled out.

"Boss says no food or drink. Truth Serum's on his way to extract information from you—and he wants you dry and hungry."

"Truth Serum is a person?" Claire asked.

"Yeah—except he doesn't use serum." Benny crossed his arms. "He likes his subjects to *bleed* the truth, if you know what I mean."

Claire swallowed dryly.

What would Max do?

Jerry slid closer to Claire—the same way a slug slimes its way across the floor, leaving a trail of ooze. He pulled open the collar of her T-shirt and peered down into her shirt.

"No food or drink – but we weren't told we couldn't loosen you up for interrogation first, though." He pouted, studying her breasts. "They're a little small for my taste."

Jerry then poured cold water down the front of Claire's shirt. She gasped, bucking uselessly to get away from the cold trickle.

"Oh, that's better," Jerry purred, studying how the cotton now plastered her shirt to her breasts, and the cold made her nipples hard and obvious. "Look how perky they are now!"

Then, he leaned in close—so close that his hot breath tentacled along her collarbone. Jerry smelled like an ashtray. He cupped her breast in one hand.

Claire rolled her head back, as if recoiling in disgust...

...and then snapped her neck sharply forward.

There was a *crunch* as Claire's forehead collided hard with Jerry's nose.

Pain shot through her skull. She blinked away tears as stars swam before her vision.

"*Merciful photon ray*," she cursed Max, who'd inspired her to try that. *Why would anyone think head-butting is an effective form of fighting?*

In all likelihood, she'd injured herself as much as Jerry.

The henchman *was* injured, though. He cried out in shock and pain, staggering backward and reaching for his bleeding nose with one hand. There was no containing the gushing waterfall of red, which poured over his fingers.

Maybe it was worth it, Claire smiled grimly—but only for a second.

"You bitch!"

Stars sprang in front of her as Jerry backhanded Claire, sending a flare of agony across her jaw. She tasted blood as pain radiated through her face. Her eyes watered.

As Jerry backed away from her, clutching his nose, Benny reached for his gun.

"Leave her!" Jerry cupped his nose. "Come help me stop the bleeding, instead." He looked towards the door. "Does this place even have an ice machine?"

The two men left the room, slamming the door shut behind them.

Claire moved her aching jaw, looking down at the blood Jerry had splattered across her shirt and pants. She made plans to burn those items as soon as she had a change of clothes. The only question was—when would that be?

Claire might have deterred Jerry's groping hands—but when he stopped the bleeding and took a few ibuprofen, he'd be back for revenge—or to finish what he'd started.

That's if the man they called Truth Serum wasn't there by then.

Sitting there alone, Claire tested the plastic ties securing her wrists to the chair. It was the hundredth time she'd tested them, and each time she rubbed her skin raw as she struggled to break free. Like all her other attempts, the ties had no give to them. She couldn't stretch them loose enough to wriggle even a hand out of them.

So, instead, Claire pushed herself to her feet—standing awkwardly with the chair still attached to her. She waddled across the room to the window.

Claire nudged the tiny, swinging lock open with her nose. It swung open a touch.

Great! Except an unlocked window provided little help if Claire couldn't physically climb through it.

She looked out of the hazy, mud-stained windowpanes at the tall pines and barren oaks trees beyond. Even if she could escape, Claire was no wilderness survivor. She wouldn't know a poisonous snake from a nonpoisonous snake—and she'd get hypothermia as soon as the sun set. In fact, wasn't there some rule about drinking water in the wild? Where you supposed to only drink from a running stream? Or only from a pool of water?

Claire didn't know. All she did know was that she'd have to steal a phone before escaping, so she could call for help; or at least search the Internet for survival tips.

But even as she considered that, her brain whirred like a computer. She studied the trees beyond the window.

Woods.

Of course, Lucius's men had taken her somewhere remote— where no one could hear her scream. Claire glanced at the shackles on the wall, betting no one had heard the screams of the last person to be held here, either.

Staring at the blood stains on the floor, she shuddered.

Suddenly, a face popped into view on the other side of the window.

Claire nearly screamed—twice.

The first time was from shock. The second was at *who'd* shocked her.

Drake!

Claire stumbled back, falling to the floor sideways. The jarring impact set her teeth rattling. She looked back at the window—but now, no one was there. Had she imagined it?

Benny suddenly burst into the room, gun drawn. He looked around the room, drawn by the sound of her stumbling.

"What happened?" He holstered his weapon.

"I tried to stand, and I fell over," Claire replied.

As Benny straightened her upright, a distant knock came from the front door. Benny drew his weapon again, walking out of the room and leaving the door open.

"Relax," she heard Jerry say through the open doorway. "It's just Drake."

"Is he supposed to be here?"

Claire heard the front door open, and then the slap of hands being clasped and the murmur of greetings being exchanged. She strained to hear their conversation.

"What're you doing here man?" Benny asked.

"Bringing beer," Drake replied in a cheerful tone.

"Sweet," Jerry said.

"You're not on this assignment," Benny said.

"Of course I am." There was the sound of a can of beer popping open. "I've been assigned to this chick since day one."

"You couldn't get the inside information," Benny said.

"That's right." Drake's voice grew seething. "I agonized through all those dates with the blue-haired freak and got *nothing*—so, now I get to be here while *she* suffers. That bitch is going to wish she'd played nice with me."

Drake's words stung. Had he been so miserable spending time with her? If that was true, he truly was a superb actor. He'd thoroughly manipulated her.

Gulps of beer were followed by a burp. "Did she do that to your nose, Jerry?"

"Bitch," Jerry snarled.

"When does the interrogator get here?" Drake's tone sounded chillingly calm—as if he was asking what time the basketball game started on television, rather than when Claire's agony would commence.

"He's on the road now—his flight into Hartsfield was delayed."

"Excellent. We have time to spare. Where's the wench?"

Jerry chuckled as heavy footsteps approached Claire's room. Drake entered, beer in hand, with Jerry trailing behind him. Benny stood in the doorway with his arms crossed, remaining just outside the room.

Claire steeled her gaze—giving Drake her most fearsome go-to-hell look.

DRAKE KNEW his performance thus far had been flawless.

He had Lucius's morons believing he was on their side. The only problem was, judging by Claire's malevolent stare, she'd bought his act, too. His heart hurt to see her like this. Claire's blue hair hung limply, framing her beautiful face—from which her eyes burned at him with cold fury.

Claire was bound to a chair in this bare room—blood stains on the floor and shackles hanging from one wall.

Drake could have kept his ruse going long enough to sneak Claire out the window—distracting Jerry and Benny with beer and the PlayStation in the next room. He'd already played the script out in his mind.

But when Drake saw Claire's appearance—one cheek red and

swollen, with blood splattered across the front of her clothing—he lost all composure.

Burning fury clutched Drake's chest. What had they done to her?

Surprising even himself, he reared back and punched Jerry hard in the face—directly on his already broken nose.

At the same time, with a roundhouse kick, Drake kicked shut the door right in Benny's shocked face.

Clutching his bloody nose, Jerry barreled toward Drake—outrage twisting his lips into a snarl. Drake didn't have time to reach for Claire's stun gun. Instead, he crouched and wrapped his arms around Jerry's waist, absorbing the impact as Lucius's henchman plowed into him. The can of beer he'd been holding skittered across the floor.

Shoving upward with his bent knees, Drake physically lifted Jerry into the air and flipped him over. Jerry struck the door behind him just as Benny flung it open again—slamming the door shut once more in Benny's face.

Still tied to the chair, Claire lashed out a leg—kicking Jerry in the face as he struggled to his knees, knocking him instantly unconscious.

Drake bent down and hefted Jerry's body against the door—knowing it wouldn't keep Benny out for long, but that they needed just sixty seconds or so to get through that window.

There was a folding knife on Jerry's belt, and Drake yanked it free—turning toward Claire. She said nothing as he sawed through the plastic ties.

As he freed her, Drake tried to assess her injuries. "Can you walk?"

"Yes. It's not my blood."

Her words of reassurance dampened his temper.

Claire began rubbing her wrists the moment they were free.

Drake straightened, ready to get Claire to safety. "I've got..."

Benny shoved the door open—pushing Jerry's unconscious body aside. The henchman stood in the doorway—a vein in his head pulsating with the strain of hefting open the barricaded door. He lifted his gun toward Drake.

Drake stood there, clutching Jerry's knife in one hand. His blood ran cold. The irony wasn't lost on him—the actor bringing a knife to a gunfight?

Benny fired.

Claire screamed.

6

laire watched in horror as Drake fell backward, shot in the gut by Benny.

At that instant, a giant animal burst through the window—charging Benny. Lucius's henchman didn't have time to adjust his aim before the dog tackled him, sinking his massive teeth into the man's forearm.

Benny's gun clattered to the floor as he unleashed a scream of pain and terror.

Bear!

Claire's heart soared to see her beloved Bullmastiff alive. She snatched the gun from the floor, before scrambling on her knees over to Drake.

He lay on his back, blank eyes staring at the ceiling.

"Drake!" Claire tore at Drake's jacket, looking for the wound. She knew First Aid, but doubted her minimal skills would suffice for a gunshot wound to the belly.

Her mind raced. She should call David—Maxine's son. He was an emergency room physician, and perhaps he could talk her through... *something*.

But then, Drake blinked and gulped in a desperate breath.

"*Sonofaminotaur*! Damn that hurts. Almost as much as the time a stage horse kicked me in the chest during a Western we were filming."

He coughed, as Claire continued to search for his injury.

Instead of a bullet wound, though, Claire's hands found something hard.

Drake unzipped one of the many pockets of his jacket and pulled out a tablet with a thick protective case. "Saved by an electronic device." He heaved out a breath.

Claire felt flush with a deluge of emotions—relief, anger, gratitude, and betrayal.

She mostly settled on betrayal—but couldn't process all her emotions right now. Instead, she pulled up the hem of Drake's jacket to see a red welt forming on his belly; but there was no puncture wound. She ran a hand along the soft skin of his firm abs. She could have lost him! Drake could have died!

Claire clambered to her feet, the stolen gun in hand. She stepped into the living room of the cabin—where Bear held Benny captive, the 130lb Bullmastiff still clamping his jaws down on Benny's arm.

"If you stop resisting," she suggested to her kidnapper, "he'll ease the pressure off the bite."

Benny stilled, panting and wide-eyed. "Can you make him stop?"

"Oh, sure—*I can*." Her eyes flashed. "But seeing as how you were planning on having me violently interrogated, I'm feeling less than generous."

Wow, Claire marveled. Suddenly, she felt like Maxine—badass, having got the upper hand and sporting a rough set of battle wounds to show for it.

Yet, despite her momentary delight, Claire knew she'd be perfectly satisfied to *never* repeat this experience—or go through anything remotely similar ever again.

I'll keep to my office and the surveillance van, thank you very much.

"Where do you keep your twist ties?"

"Drawer in the kitchen, beside the refrigerator," Benny responded through clenched teeth. His eyes watered as Bear kept him in his grasp.

By the time Claire found the twist ties, Drake was back on his feet. He walked into the living room just as Claire tossed him the strands of plastic.

"Tag 'em and bag 'em."

With the gun trained on Benny, Claire gave Bear instructions to heel. When the massive dog finally released the man from his vice-like jaws, Drake was on hand to restrain Benny.

With the two kidnappers bound wrist and ankle, Claire finally handed Drake the gun—before bending over to wrap her arms around Bear.

"Good boy," she nuzzled the big, slobbery dog's ears. "You're *such* a good boy."

"Claire?"

She looked up at Drake.

"You can have your reunion in the car. We gotta go—*now!*" Drake's voice was half-pleading, half-compassionate.

Claire stood. "Fine—but you and I are *not* okay."

He rubbed his stomach. "I took a bullet for you."

"You took a bullet for *you*."

"What about *me*?" Benny complained, rolled up on the floor.

"You want a bullet?" Claire asked, confused.

"No! This bite wound! It could get infected."

Claire shrugged. "Truth Serum will be here soon. I'm sure he's real compassionate about injuries—especially when his intended victim gets away."

Benny's eyes widened in realization. He and Jerry would be found here tied up, and without Claire. Their failure wouldn't bode well for their future with Titan Enterprises.

⁂

DRAKE HIT the gas and spun his Explorer around the driveway. Gravel scattered in an arch behind the vehicle, evidenced by the sound of rocks clattering across the house and the other vehicles.

His heart still raced from the adrenaline of battle, but Drake kept the SUV steady as he turned onto the highway.

He'd used the knife to puncture Jerry's tires, so Lucius's goons couldn't follow them if they got free—but that didn't mean they had time to dawdle. The man they called Truth Serum could arrive at any moment.

As he glanced in the rearview mirror, Drake glimpsed Claire staring out of the window—one hand protectively on Bear, and the other gripping the bar above the window. Bear occupied the entire rest of the bench seat—lying with his big head in Claire's lap.

Lucky dog.

Drake thought of the way Claire's hands had run over his abdomen, as she'd assessed his potential injury. He remembered seeing her brow knit with worry.

Then, he remembered her warning: "You and I are *not* okay."

Shifting in his seat, Drake turned his attention back to the road. "By the way, Claire—this is Pete."

Pete, who'd remained in the passenger seat, gave Claire a shy wave, obviously sensing the tension between Drake and Claire.

"Pete, meet Claire. Claire, meet Pete."

"Your dog woke up and went crazy," Pete explained. "I hope it's okay I let him out of the car."

"Yes—and thank you." Claire studied the stranger. "What is it you do, Pete? I only ask because Drake here poses as an actor while spying on people—*and* he works for one of the worst, most life-sucking humans on the planet."

Pete grimaced. "Drake's *actually* an actor. He's posing as a private security agent."

Claire never stopped talking, but she turned her heated words toward Drake. "I trusted you, Drake. I went to a *football* game with you."

Drake grit his teeth. Claire could show some gratitude, since he'd risked his life to rescue her. "Well, I went to Comic Con, so we're even."

That was petty. He'd actually enjoyed the quirky event, since he'd been in Claire's company. She'd been so excited to take pictures on a mock set, matching the bridge of the Starship Enterprise. Claire had worn a tight, leather outfit and red wig—dressed as the Black Widow from *The Avengers*. She'd been radiant and mouth-watering—and her youthful exuberance had made Drake feel ten years younger.

That was just one of the many interactions with Claire which had solidified his conviction that he'd never betray her—and kept him desperately wondering how he could possibly wriggle out of his position in Lucius Titan's organization.

From the passenger seat, Pete cleared his throat.

Shit.

"You went to a *comic convention*? With Claire?" Pete's voice was woven with pain and betrayal. "How could you, man?"

Drake winced. "I'm sorry, Pete."

"All those years I asked you, and you *never* went with me."

Drake glanced in the rearview mirror again, watching Claire's lips quirk a moment before she turned and looked back out of the window.

He didn't think explaining the difference between going to Comic Con with a guy friend—as opposed to a fully-costumed, beautiful woman—would do anything to smooth things over with either Pete or Claire; so Drake kept quiet.

As Drake drove, Pete turned in his seat to look at Claire. "You hate football?"

"I don't *hate* it."

Drake sighed. "She finds it abhorrent that a civilized society would fund a billion-dollar industry which provides entertainment in the form of men beating each other up over a pigskin ball —all while scantily-dressed women shake more than just pom-poms and cheer them on."

He didn't have to see Claire's face to know she'd shot him an incredulous look.

"Yes, sweetheart," his tone was bitter, "I *was* paying attention."

Who could blame him for being bitter? He'd been fighting for his life fifteen minutes earlier. Now, he was in the doghouse with both of them.

"Well, sorry you wasted your time," Claire hissed. "We're *done*."

Claire's words stung, but Drake wouldn't let her know she'd hurt him.

"Yeah," he admitted. "I kinda figured that when you slammed my car door shut as you left." He sighed raggedly. "Well, at least I got you out of the mess I put you in—so, I guess I'm done as well. As soon as I drop you back at your place, I'm riding off into the sunset."

With Pete.

Drake frowned.

That wasn't the '*hasta-la-vista, baby*' image he'd been hoping to conjure up.

Beside him in the passenger seat, Pete's expression turned doleful as he addressed Claire. "Listen, Drake didn't know how bad Titan Enterprises was—*is*. He thought if he worked for a private security company for a little while, it would help his acting career. He just wanted some real-work experience—to be like Jason Statham in *The Transporter* movies."

"Well," Claire shot back, "his acting seems fine enough already. He certainly did a job with it on me." She snorted bitterly. "If I didn't know any better, I'd have thought he actually gave a damn about me. Instead, I was just a job."

Drake gripped the wheel tightly, saying nothing.

What was there to say?

"Listen, it's my fault," Pete pleaded. "I created a fake military background file for Drake—the one which got him hired at Titan Enterprises."

"How did HR *not* pick up it was fake?" Claire asked.

Pete shrugged. "I picked commanding officers who'd died in service. Titan's human resources didn't have anyone to refute or deny the information."

"Sloppy—on Titan's part, I mean."

"Yeah." Pete ran his hands over his ruined tablet, mumbling his disbelief. "I can't believe they shot my tablet."

"I wouldn't have stopped with the military records," Claire said. "I'd have dug deeper. I personally vet every Rider employee —no imposters would get past me."

Drake caught Pete glancing at him.

Claire gave a bitter laugh at the exchanged looks. "Okay, yeah —no imposters *except* my date. If I'd applied my work tactics to my dating tactics, I'd have caught Drake in the lie."

Drake continued to stew in silence. He hadn't meant to deceive

Claire—and most of the time he'd spent with her had been voluntary and real.

But there'd be no convincing her of that now. The two of them would be better off after they parted ways.

Miles rumbled beneath the tires of Drake's Explorer.

In the back seat, Claire stared out the window, chewing her lip. The fear of the kidnapping and the fatigue of spending hours tied to that chair continued to make her irritable. Part of her wanted to scream at Drake—but, much to her frustration, part of her just wanted to tear the clothes off him and wrap her legs around his waist.

Whoa—where had *that* come from?

Claire felt her cheeks burn hotly. She brushed a snarled strand of blue hair from her face, shivering. It must be the sleep deprivation—that's all.

"Where are we headed?" Pete inquired.

"Like I said—Claire's place."

"What I meant to ask was: Is her place safe?"

"I've got people," Claire said.

"There you have it," Drake gestured to Claire, while talking to Pete. "She has people. She'll be fine."

Pete pulled Drake's phone from the center console and handed it to Claire. "Do you need to call your people?"

Claire snatched the phone and began dialing. "Yes. Thanks." She disconnected the speakers from the car's Bluetooth.

Nevertheless, Maxine's angry voice was loud enough to be recognized even without the amplification of Drake's radio. "You better be calling me with good news, Fitzy, because if you've screwed this up…"

"Max—it's Claire."

"*Thank God*! Claire, where are you? What happened? Are you safe? Drake called me and said Titan's men took you."

Claire felt a wave of relief to hear Maxine Rider's gruff voice. Tears prickled Claire's eyes, but she refused to cry—not around Max, and *certainly* not in front of Drake. "I'm out. I'm safe. I'm on my way home."

"Head toward Mica's safe house."

"Okay." The cabin belonging to Mica's father made sense. It would be an hour's drive west—now that Claire knew geographically where she was—and closer than going all the way back to Atlanta.

"You know what that means, right? Batteries out of your cell phones."

"I know," Claire sniffed.

"Claire, are you hurt?" The worry in Maxine's voice was palpable. It left Claire wanting a hug from her surly boss.

"No."

Not physically. Claire glanced up at Drake.

He was the reason she was currently safe. He'd rescued her—despite having no genuine military background. Drake had risked his life when he hadn't had to.

But, still—he'd *lied* to her, even after she'd thought a romantic relationship was starting to blossom between them.

"Are you alone?" Maxine suddenly asked.

Maxine must have correctly gleaned from Claire's short, gruff answers that she was with other people.

"No."

"But you're safe?"

"Yes."

A pause, then. "Is Drake Fitzgerald with you?"

"Yes."

"You tell that pissant sonofa..."

Claire held the phone away from her ear as Maxine swore fluently enough to make a sailor proud.

"Max! Max! Okay, calm down!" Claire interrupted her boss. "We're headed your way. I'm powering down."

"Stay safe."

Claire ended the call with Maxine. After sending a text message to Mica, confirming her safety, Claire took out the cell phone battery and killed the phone.

Mica would be disappointed not to get a verbal call, but Claire knew she wouldn't be able to maintain her composure if she spoke to her best friend.

"Phone." It was a command, aimed at Pete.

"Are you planning on dismantling my phone, too?"

"Yes—batteries out. We need to go to one of the team's safe houses, and we need to ensure we're not traced there."

Drake glanced briefly back at Claire. "Forget that! How many times have you told me Max protects her own? I'm pretty sure the cussing we all heard was directed at me."

Claire smirked. "You scared?"

"Of Maxine Rider? Damn right I am! Even the guys at Titan Enterprises are scared of her."

"Fine. Drop me off at a gas station. I'll have one of the team pick me up and take me to the safe house, instead."

Claire could see Drake clenching his teeth. For several moments, only the sound of the vehicle's engine and the rumbling tires filled the Explorer.

Finally, Claire asked: "Drake?"

"I'm not dropping you off somewhere," he snapped. Dread had replaced anger in Drake's tone. He snatched Pete's phone from him and handed it over his shoulder to Claire. "I'll deliver you safely to Maxine."

As Claire took the phone, her fingers brushed Drake's. She ignored the flutter skittering through her chest as their skin touched.

It wasn't real, she angrily reminded herself. None of it was ever real.

"One more thing," she said. "We need to blindfold Pete."

———

Mica pulled over at a Dollar General store and stared at her phone. From an unknown number, she'd received a message from Claire—telling Mica she was free from captivity, and giving a list of items she'd hoped Mica could bring to the safe house for her.

Mica felt relief—but when she tried calling the number, it went straight to voicemail—Drake Fitzgerald's voicemail.

Mica then called Maxine, who confirmed that she'd spoken directly with Claire and that she was safe.

A pang of disappointment struck Mica that Claire hadn't called her directly.

Once Mica hung up with Maxine, she started making a mental list of all the people she'd need to update. Mason Stone was first—one of Rider SI employees currently working with Dorian Chaplin on a missing persons case in Louisiana.

"Mica? What's the word?" Mason had demanded the moment he'd picked up the call.

"Claire's safe." Mica spoke as she navigated the Target, dumping items into her cart. This included a change of clothes for both of them—plus a comfortable pair of shoes. Mica had been wound as tight as a spring since Maxine had told her about Claire's kidnapping. At last, she could uncoil—which included making the rest of her drive in comfortable, cushioned sneakers.

Mason responded, "Thank God. What's the next move?"

"Tonight, we rest. We let Claire rest. Tomorrow, we'll calculate our next move."

"But we're going to strike back, right? Maxine *is* planning retaliation?" Mason's tone was insistent.

Mica could envision the tall, robust man pacing back and forth, running a hand through his shaggy, blond hair.

Lucius's blow had been below the belt—but it had also made each team member acutely aware of how vulnerable they all were. What if it hadn't been Claire who Lucius had targeted? What if it had been one of their loved ones?

The first thing Mica had done after Maxine had called her earlier was to check in with David and make sure he was safe. Mica couldn't stomach the thought of anything happening to the love of her life.

As for Mason? He'd no doubt be thinking of his wife, Aurora Meridian. She traveled in the women's professional tennis circuit. Lucius had previously proven that his reach extended internationally. That meant Mason could be an ocean away from his wife when Aurora needed him the most.

"We *will* retaliate," Mica assured Mason in a calm voice, "but we're not going to rush anything and be careless."

"Okay. I like the sound of that."

"How's your case going?" Mica asked.

"Following the breadcrumbs. You need me to come back?"

"No. Finish the job—but Max and I may need to pull Dorian."

"He's a good partner, but I understand under the circumstances."

"He has a unique skill set we might need," Mica added.

"Understood."

After ending the call with Mason, Mica updated Billy and Barry, who were also elsewhere on assignment. The last call Mica made was to Bill Sharp—the Rider SI's client who Mica was currently assigned to, and the one who she'd left abruptly earlier that day.

"Bill Sharp."

"Mr. Sharp? It's Mica. I'm calling from a burner phone. I'm sorry I had to run out today on such short notice."

"No problem. Is Claire okay?"

"She's okay. She's safe now."

"Good. I've been worried. I remember the time she toured my R & D facility not long after I hired Maxine Rider. Claire was simply dazzled by my toys. There's seldom anything more flattering than someone with genuine interest and knowledge about my creations." He snorted. "Claire's smart as a whip when it comes to technology."

"She's our computer genius," Mica admitted.

"You still think Lucius Titan is behind the kidnapping?"

"It's confirmed now," she said.

Bill made a noise, which sounded part-grunt and part-growl. He had his own reasons for disliking Lucius, ever since the head of Titan Enterprises had tried to steal his drone prototypes last year. "What's the recourse?"

"Retaliation. In fact, Max might want me running point on a few aspects as we plan our next move. My time on your detail may be affected."

"You've made strides with my personnel in a few short months. We'll manage if you need to multitask."

"Thank you, Mr. Sharp."

7

—————

Claire scrutinized the cabin as Drake parked his car behind Maxine's vehicle.

The wood exterior was a gorgeous pine, peaking at a steep roof. Through a large window, she could see the living room within, lit by a medieval-looking metal chandelier and a large fireplace. She'd never seen this safe house before. In fact, she'd never seen any of Maxine's safe houses before.

Claire worked in the office—supposedly safe and comfortable behind a desk. She'd never been a part of the danger of the Rider teams' lives before. Now, she was wading neck-deep in it.

She climbed out of the backseat of Drake's Explorer and held the door as Bear leapt down and began sniffing the premises. Her body felt stiff and sore, and her shirt reeked of blood and body odor. She wanted nothing more than to soak in a tub—but knew the first order of business would be a debriefing with Maxine.

Claire closed the car door and waited as Bear relieved himself under a nearby tree. So many dense trees, she noted—and the quiet of the forest felt utterly complete.

Claire was accustomed to the bustling metropolis of Atlanta—sirens, horns, and diesel truck engines. The silence in these north Georgia mountains was simultaneously relaxing and eerie.

As she walked up the porch stairs, with Drake, Pete, and Bear in tow, Claire glanced at the other vehicles in the gravel driveway. There was Maxine's Crossover and Ryan's Explorer.

Claire knocked twice and the door swung open. Maxine hauled her inside, enveloping her in a rough hug.

Wow, she must have really been worried!

Maxine seldom hugged. As the former Marine spun Claire away from the door and into the kitchen, Claire realized her boss wasn't hugging her—she was whisking her away from the men accompanying her.

Ryan Walsh and Reece Owen swooped in like stealth bombers, training their handguns on Drake and Pete the moment Claire was out of the firing line.

"Whoa, whoa, whoa!" Pete threw up his hands. "We're the good guys here."

Drake raised his hands slowly and quietly. He seemed resigned to whatever fate he was destined to meet at the hands of the Rider team.

As Reece kept his gun leveled at Drake and Pete, Ryan began frisking them. He started with Pete, who was shaking with fear.

"It's okay, Max," Claire explained, looking over her shoulder at her two rescuers. "They saved me."

Ryan finished frisking Pete, and then moved on to Drake.

Patting down his jacket, he found Claire's stun gun, Drake's disabled cell phone, a pack of gum, three pens, two flash drives...

"*For crying out loud*! How many damned pockets does this thing have?" Ryan's dark eyes flashed.

Pete, hands still in the air, replied, "Seventeen."

Ryan stepped back, shaking his head. "Just take the damn thing off."

Drake obliged, moving gingerly and eyeing Reece's gun as he removed the jacket Pete had loaned him.

After Ryan had finished checking Drake, Maxine lunged for him—and she wasn't pulling any punches. The former Marine *slammed* Drake against one wall—pinning him against it with one arm pressed against his throat.

Drake let out a grunt of surprise and pain, but didn't resist her assault. He gasped for air, looking at his assailant with a mixture of fear and awe. "You must be Maxine Rider."

"Max!" Claire cried. "He rescued me!"

"He works for Titan."

"Yes, he *did*—and it was a mistake." Claire avoided eye contact with Drake, so she didn't have to see his look of surprise as she defended him. Sure, Claire harbored justifiable anger and frustration toward him, but she didn't want Maxine's wrath unleashed on the man who'd saved her life.

Pete, meanwhile, watched the display with wide eyes—his mouth gaping open.

"Max," Claire laid a reassuring hand on Maxine's shoulder, and spoke softly, "When Drake learned what kind of business Titan Enterprises actually is, he flipped sides." She lowered her voice, murmuring: "Let him go, Max."

For a moment, Maxine just stood there, crushing Drake against the wall.

Eventually, with a snarl of frustration, Maxine released Drake.

He staggered back, reaching for his throat as he gasped for air. His red face began to return to a normal color.

With that crisis resolved, Ryan pulled Claire into a hug—a *real* hug, this time.

"We were so worried about you!"

Claire leaned into the embrace, absorbing the strength Ryan radiated.

"I'm okay."

Reece, meanwhile, bent down to pet Bear. "I was more worried about the dog." When Claire shot him a glare, Reece winked at her —gently stroking behind the dog's ears.

Her irritation immediately subsided. Claire chuckled at Reece as she straightened and composed herself. "If you care so much— can you get him some water?"

"Sure thing." Reece walked to the kitchen and filled a bowl.

Claire turned back to Max. "Just let Drake leave, Max—and his friend, Pete. He isn't even a part of this."

Max narrowed her eyes at the pair of them.

"He is now," she warned. "Neither of you boys can leave this safe house until we have a plan to *eliminate* Titan." Then she snarled, "...and lower your damn hands. You look ridiculous."

Pete dropped his hands to his side.

Claire stepped up behind her boss. "You can't just hold them hostage, Max."

"The hell I can't," she snapped back. "Fitzy here has compromised the security of my entire team."

"We both know Titan was bound to come after one of us eventually—and he's already tried to get to your son."

"I intend to do what I *need* to do, in order to keep my team safe." Maxine fired back.

Claire stomped her foot. "Fine! Keep him—but stop *blaming* him."

"Why?"

"Because you're forcing me to defend him, and it's pissing me off!"

The corner of Maxine's lip turned up in something similar to a grin.

Before she could speak again, though, footsteps sounded on the porch—causing everyone to flinch.

"At ease." Reece glanced out of the window. "It's Mica."

When Ryan opened the door, Mica rushed into the room and embraced Claire. "*Heavens*! I was worried about you." She pulled away and inspected Claire's face. "You've been hit."

Claire touched a hand to her swollen cheekbone. She laughed dryly. "You should see the other guy. No, really—I busted his nose!"

Mica shook off a laugh, her blonde curls swinging around her head. She wore a skirt suit, making Claire suspect she'd come to the cabin directly from work, where she was currently assigned to help Bill Sharp—a weapons developer—keep his drone prototypes safe.

Mica cocked her head to one side and regarded Drake. "Is this the dickhead?"

Claire stepped protectively between them. "Yes—but Max has already indoctrinated him."

Mica scrutinized Drake, as if making her own determination as to whether Claire's would-be boyfriend had been physically accosted enough. Mica might have the appearance of beauty and glamour—but the martial arts expert was every bit as tough and resourceful a fighter as Ryan Walsh.

From the expression on her face, it appeared that Mica wasn't satisfied with the treatment Drake had received—but she decided against making any additional move against him.

Maxine's voice rang out across the cabin. "I need a drink. Claire needs rest. Everybody at ease." She turned and left.

Mica glanced at Claire. "I bought you some toiletries and clothes—*and* the thing you texted me about."

Claire loved her Rider family. "Thank you." She hugged Mica again.

⸺ ⸱ ⸺

LUCIUS RELISHED the feel of warm, agile, and feminine hands on his back. The massage therapist worked her lubricated fingers deep into his muscles. A calming lavender scent infused the air. Whenever he took the time for his weekly massage, Lucius always wondered why he didn't schedule this necessary luxury daily.

Then he remembered. It was because he worked twelve-hour days, and didn't want to stretch them out even longer.

Since his masseuse was one of the women AJ had plucked from their human trafficking chain, Lucius had the pleasure of culminating the tranquil experience with what most would refer to as a 'happy ending'.

He felt no guilt about it. His masseuse was one of the lucky ones—a stolen woman, now living in a gilded cage in exchange for obediently servicing him or his clients whenever she was expected to. To the woman's credit, she was subservient and appropriately grateful about her new circumstances. Lucius told himself he'd probably saved her from a life of poverty back in Croatia.

It was more than a fair exchange. Oh, those caressing hands of hers... The only thing more pleasurable than their touch was that of the woman's silky tongue.

Lucius's phone rang.

Swearing, he reached up and tapped his Bluetooth earpiece. If it had been anyone other than Hoyle, he'd have let it go to voicemail.

"Titan."

"It's Hoyle. Claire Maltisse got away."

Lucius bolted upright on the massage table. "Maxine Rider found her? *How*?" Lucius had specifically instructed the buffoons who'd grabbed Claire to leave her phone behind, and search for any additional tracking devices she might have concealed.

"No, it wasn't Maxine Rider," Hoyle explained nervously. "Benny and Jerry say Drake Rivera showed up and took them both out."

"Drake? Drake, the pretty-boy, wannabe actor with no actual military background? He took out two former Army infantry?" The massage therapist stepped behind Lucius and began gently rubbing his neck, but Lucius waved her away with irritation.

Lucius had become aware of Drake's true identity only a few days earlier. Until then, he'd had no reason to question Drake's service record—not until one of Lucius's men had questioned the veracity of Drake's military background. He'd noticed that Drake wasn't familiar with the military lingo most of the Titan employees used.

Lucius had his human resources people dig deeper—and they weren't able to verify a single element of the military training and experience Drake Rivera claimed to have.

There was, however, another 'Drake' they'd uncovered. Facial recognition had flagged a certain 'Drake Fitzgerald' during their search—a B actor from Los Angeles who was physically identical to the Titan employee calling himself Drake Rivera.

In subsequent searches, HR had found no connection between Drake Fitzgerald and Maxine Rider—or any other of Lucius's enemies—but they were undeniably the same individual.

Initially, Lucius had been unconcerned. As far as he'd been aware, none of his operations had been compromised as a result of this deception. Nevertheless, Drake Rivera had been promptly fired for falsifying his application and his access to the Titan Enterprises building had been immediately terminated. That should have been the end of it—and the imposter hadn't attempted to return to work.

But word hadn't yet spread across Titan Enterprises that Drake had been fired, since Human Resources had performed his termination quietly in an attempt not to draw attention to their egregious mistake.

In fact, Hoyle had been one of the few Titan employees to know that HR had inadvertently hired an actor—but he'd been too busy to pay Drake the customary visit that all terminated Titan employees received: During which they'd be warned that sharing anything confidential they'd learned during their employment with Titan Enterprises would result in consequences that went significantly—and painfully—beyond mere legal recourse.

"Drake had the element of surprise."

So, as far as most Titan Employees knew, Drake had still been on the payroll—and that explained what Hoyle told Lucius.

"But he didn't even know about the cabin!" Lucius growled, and then angrily shook his head. "Never mind."

Lucius couldn't undo the damage done. He needed to push forward, instead. He'd have to think of another way to get at Maxine.

"Did Truth Serum arrive?"

"Yeah. He wants to know if he's still going to get paid."

"Tell him I have another job for him. I'll text him the details."

Securing the Bluetooth earpiece, Lucius walked to his minibar —still naked from his massage. He poured himself a Scotch and added a splash of water.

Hoyle asked, "What do you want me to do with Benny and Jerry?"

Lucius took a gulp of his drink.

"Do to them what we do to all of those who fail me."

Through the earpiece, Lucius heard sudden, desperate protests—followed by two loud, ominous gunshots. Then, silence.

Lucius reached up and pulled off his earpiece, before turning his hard gaze towards the masseuse. "Bend over. I'm taking my damn happy ending."

CLAIRE MIXED the hair dye according to the directions.

She was glad Mica had fulfilled the request she'd sent in her text message—the one before she'd had to pull the battery from Drake's phone. Mica had selected hair coloring for her, and now Claire massaged the dark liquid into the roots of her blue-dyed hair.

As the chemicals sat in her hair, she looked at her pale face in the mirror. The only color in her complexion came from the ugly bruises on her jaw and the peak of her forehead.

There was a knock on the bathroom door.

"Claire?"

Claire opened the door and found Maxine standing there. She let her boss into the small bathroom and received a glass of whisky in return.

Claire sniffed the toxic liquid. "I don't drink that stuff."

"Today you do. Just one shot—it'll help with the jitters and let you sleep."

Claire chocked back the drink, which was followed by an uncomfortable burning sensation through her throat, nose, and eyes. "Ugh! I think I'd rather perform another headbutt than drink this rocket fuel."

"You *headbutted* someone?"

Claire felt proud of Maxine's reaction. "Yeah—but I think it hurt me as much as it did him, so I'm not sure I did it right."

Maxine chuckled as she took the now-empty glass from Claire. She leaned against the bathroom counter, careful to avoid the drips of hair coloring.

"You want to talk about it?"

Claire wasn't sure if Maxine's hesitant tone was because she didn't want to hear the details—or because she didn't want Claire to become upset by reliving those events.

"Not really."

Events.

Those events had only happened a few hours ago—and Claire wasn't yet prepared to share the fear she'd felt during her experience. That fear still scoured her raw, clinging to her like the blood on her clothing.

Maxine stuck her hand in the pocket of her cargo pants. "Changing your hair color?"

"Yeah. I felt like I needed a change."

"I can understand that. After my first tour with the Marines, I got back to the States on leave, put on a dress, and I picked up a guy at a bar."

Claire lifted her head, eyes widening at Maxine's confession.

She didn't seem ashamed about it. "I just needed to feel alive after witnessing so much death—some of which I'd caused."

Claire blinked at Maxine. She seldom talked about her past. Claire hadn't killed anyone, but she understood the parallel Maxine was trying to make—and appreciated it.

She gestured towards the box of hair dye Mica had bought for her. "Well, this is just hair color—I'm not going to any bars and sleeping with strangers any time soon."

Maxine laughed dryly. "Wasn't all bad. I got David out of it."

"You met your husband at a bar?"

"*Ex*-husband," Maxine clarified, "and yes. We met, we fell in love, we had David—and then we fell out of love."

"And now, you have Vlad." Claire thought she'd push her luck a little, since Maxine seemed to be in a rare, talkative mood—sharing the enigma of her past.

"Yes," Maxine's face hardened slightly. "I'm clearly not a role model here, since I'm both divorced *and* now dating a Russian mobster."

Claire laughed. "A role model for relationships? No. But you *are* a role model for determination and perseverance, which is what I need right now."

"Whatever you're feeling about the shit you just went through —*feel it,*" Maxine urged. "Your feelings aren't wrong, and they don't make you weak. Let them wash over you—the fear, anger, and vulnerability. They're all normal things to feel when your life is threatened. Experience them at your own pace."

Claire sniffed and nodded.

"Okay. Let's do this hug thing—I hear it works sometimes."

To Claire's surprise, Maxine pulled her into her arms.

Mama Maxine, Claire thought.

This tough Marine was the closest thing Claire had to a caring mother—and she truly appreciated her. Claire's own biological mother had been an inner city crack-cocaine user. Claire had become the responsible one at the age of eight—mother to her own mother. When Claire had left for college at seventeen, she'd never looked back.

Her eyes suddenly flooded. Claire let the tears flow down her cheeks as Maxine hugged her tightly, patting her on the back in a reassuring, if somewhat awkward gesture. Somehow, Maxine's awkwardness made this moment all the more special.

The electronic timer on Claire's new, untraceable phone suddenly began beeping.

"Time's up." She pulled away from Maxine. "I need to rinse."

Maxine took a step back, placing one hand on the doorknob. "Rest tonight, Claire. Tomorrow, we'll start plotting our revenge against Lucius."

She left, closing the door behind her.

Claire turned on the taps, letting warm water deluge into the sink. As she watched it, she pondered Maxine's words.

Revenge.

Part of her didn't want revenge. Vengeance wasn't part of Claire's composition. What she really wanted was a month—or maybe twelve—all to herself, preferably on some tropical island, forgetting the events of the past twelve hours.

Perhaps Claire contemplated revenge on Jerry—but she already sensed he'd be sufficiently reprimanded by Lucius for allowing her to escape.

Instead of revenge, Claire mostly just wanted to *never* see Jerry, or Benny, or Hoyle ever again.

But the plotting they now needed to do against Lucius Titan would take precedence over Claire's desire to leave this experience behind her.

They needed to take him down, *now*—before Lucius went after another Rider team member. Knowing the atrocities Lucius had committed, Rider SI should have probably taken him down a lot sooner; but fulfilling the needs of their clients and keeping everyone productive and employed had taken precedence over expensive, offensive action against a significantly more powerful adversary.

Claire spoke to herself in the mirror as she peered at her slick, dye-filled hair.

"Well, as pep talks go, that was one of Max's better ones."

She turned on the shower, stripping down to step into the warm water and tossing her dirty clothes in the trash can.

The steaming streams washed away the cold Claire still felt from the hours she'd spent tied up in that cabin, which had seeped deep into her bones. When Claire eventually stopped shivering, she also stopped feeling sorry for herself. She was simply exhausted.

On autopilot, she washed the rest of the dye from her scalp, toweled off, and dried her newly colored hair. When she eventually climbed into bed, Claire had the reassurance of knowing she was safely surrounded by Bear at the foot of her bed and a half-dozen friends—all armed to the teeth to defend her.

8

*D*rake woke the next morning to the smell of eggs and chorizo.

He'd showered the night before and, since he didn't have an overnight bag, he'd borrowed a shirt from Pete to sleep in.

They'd shared a room in this remote cabin—but hadn't spoken much the night before. Pete was lamenting his destroyed tablet and the fact that he had no access to electronic devices to help him decompress. In fact, Ryan Walsh had confiscated all of Drake and Pete's digital gadgets—so none of them could be used them to trace the Rider SI team here. Drake had apologized to Pete as they'd laid in their beds, staring up at the ceiling.

It was ironic. How many times had Drake imagined sleeping

under the same roof as Claire? One thing was certain—none of the scenarios he'd imagined had ever looked like this.

With the sunlight peeking around the edges of the curtains, Drake pulled on his blue jeans, freshened up, and readied himself to face the Rider team.

When he joined them in the kitchen, which opened to the connecting living room, he sensed they'd been up for a while.

The broad-shouldered Ryan and the Marilyn Monroe-like Mica looked to be several cups of coffee deep into the morning already. Maxine sat in a recliner by the crackling fireplace, looking contemplative.

Drake stepped past them, opting to avoid direct eye contact with anyone.

Then, he saw Claire.

She was leaning on the kitchen counter, sitting in a bar stool and wearing cotton shorts and a fitted T-shirt. Her hair was now a silky, jet black—complementing her fair skin. Drake forced himself not to stare. She'd been cute with blue hair, but she looked beautiful with that striking glossy, black hair.

But the attraction Drake felt for her didn't matter. Claire despised him, and he was leaving—right after one cup of coffee.

He stepped into the kitchen and poured the last cup into a mug. He set to work making another pot—certain the Rider SI team would be needing it. He might have made a life-threatening error in judgment by working for Lucius—and endangered Claire's life in the process—but he still had manners.

If you take the last cup, you make the next pot.

As Drake pressed the filter paper in the coffee maker, he noted egg, cheese, and chorizo on the counter, waiting for the next person to make his or her breakfast. His stomach growled. He hadn't eaten since much earlier the day before—when he'd turned up to find Claire's house empty and Bear slumbering on the floor.

However, considering the doghouse he was in, Drake certainly *wasn't* going to cook himself a leisurely breakfast—not with the Rider team glaring at him. Instead, he just added half-and-half to his coffee—hoping that would suffice for calories until he left the cabin.

He leaned against the counter and looked up at Claire.

Her long, dark lashes matched her now dark hair. She still had that bruise on her jaw, but it was now partially covered with make-up. Her hands were wrapped around a cup of steaming, green tea.

"Are you okay?"

Claire glanced up at him, not looking anything like the fragile fairy he'd seen her as when he'd burst into that cabin and found her tied to the chair.

One thing was certain—Claire was tougher than he'd ever been.

Eventually, she replied: "I'm okay."

He gestured towards her mug.

"Let me warm that up for you."

To Drake's relief, she relinquished the cup without protest. As he turned to the microwave, the continued weight of all those eyes pressed down on him. He'd played parts in movies in which he'd felt under less scrutiny.

Well, they'd be rid of him soon enough—both Rider SI *and* Claire.

When the microwave eventually dinged, Drake retrieved the mug and dipped Claire's tea bag back into the hot water. He stared at the steaming liquid as it turned a deeper honey color, tinged with a faint green tint.

He'd miss Claire.

A strange ache settled in Drake's chest at the thought that he'd soon drive away from this cabin—and likely never see Claire again.

He'd never make her a cup of tea again. There'd be no more Comic Cons, or another dog walk in the park.

With a sigh, he handed the reheated tea back to her.

Claire hated him, he reminded himself. There was no point in getting upset over a one-sided relationship. Instead, he drank his coffee under the awkward stares and glares of the Rider team.

Pete finally shuffled into the room, still dressed in his pajamas. His bushy hair sprawled in all directions, even more untamed than usual. "Whoa. Bunch of early risers."

"It's already eight o'clock, Pete," Drake noted.

"I know, so early—and I'm still on Pacific time." Pete yawned as he walked to the refrigerator and poured himself a glass of orange juice.

"So, what's the plan?" Pete asked Drake, as he shut the fridge door. "Claire's safe. She's back with her peeps." As if noticing her standing there for the first time, Pete waved. "Morning Claire."

Claire waved back.

"Are we going back to your place?" Pete continued obliviously. "Do I get my cell phone and computer back now?" He turned to Drake. "You owe me a new tablet, by the way—but I'm keeping the old one, so I can show friends how my jacket saved your life."

Maxine stood, coffee mug in hand. "Nobody goes home," she warned. "I can't have either of you sharing information with Titan."

"We blindfolded Pete for the ride here," Claire said. "He's just an ignorant bystander." She turned to Pete and clarified with a sheepish grin, "I meant that in a good way."

"I *am* ignorant." He lifted his glass of juice into the air, making a cheerful toast.

"Blindfolded, huh?" Maxine poured herself a cup of coffee from the fresh batch Drake had just brewed. She turned to him. "Then, that leaves you—the *semi*-ignorant one."

Drake swallowed as he faced Maxine's steely blue eyes. She was like a female Clint Eastwood—all-seeing, all-knowing, and all-kick your ass seven ways to Sunday.

Although she looked up at him, and he looked down at her, he still felt like a weather-beaten Odysseus beneath a towering Athena.

When Claire had blindfolded Pete in the car, Drake understood why. He'd also suspected there would be consequences to not being blindfolded himself.

But that had been a choice, even if it wasn't one he'd been aware of making at the time. Drake could have asked Claire to blindfold him, too—so the Rider SI team would have no excuse to make him stick around—but he hadn't.

Drake straightened up. "I'm not going to tell Lucius anything about your team."

Maxine scrutinized his face. "I believe you wouldn't *willingly*." She took a sip of her coffee. "But I can't take the chance Titan might snatch you and force his puppet to talk."

Drake bristled at the insult.

"Besides," Maxine continued, "that rescue mission of yours painted a target on your own back, too—so, we'll make an exchange, instead." She leaned in closer. "In exchange for you staying under the radar by staying with the Rider team, you're going to be Claire's new bodyguard."

Protests erupted among the Rider team. Everyone rose to their feet.

"Are you kidding? *I'll* protect Claire," Ryan said.

Claire put her hands on her hips and gaped at Maxine. "You can't be serious!"

"Max, you don't put a rookie rider in an arena full of bulls," Reece snapped.

"Yeah! He's the one who almost got her killed," Mica added.

Through all of this, Drake remained silent—absorbing each of their reactions. Of all the objections, Claire's had stung Drake the most. Why *wouldn't* Maxine be serious? Why *couldn't* Drake be her bodyguard? He'd been a stunt double for ten years. He knew

Aikido, Jujitsu, Taekwondo, and Karate. He knew how to shoot firearms—almost any type of firearm, and although he'd never used live ammunition on set, he'd fired plenty of live rounds at the gun range as part of his research into various weapons. He wasn't military trained, like his fake resume to Titan had claimed, but he still knew he could shoot a dead-center headshot with a .22 at seventy feet—and he also knew you'd better have damn good aim with a .22, because a nonfatal shot would only piss off a determined attacker.

Likewise, Drake knew a .45 caliber packed a hell of a kick—and he hadn't used an indoor shooting range when he'd been test firing those, so as not to risk going deaf even with earmuffs.

Hell, he even knew that an AK-47 assault rifle weighed just under ten pounds, fired up to six hundred rounds a minute, and had a maximum effective range of about twelve hundred feet; because he'd spent a weekend in Nevada shooting one.

When Maxine raised her hand, everyone fell quiet.

One by one, she addressed them. "Ryan, you *are* going to be a part of Claire's protection detail—but I also need you watching Lucius. You can't be with her 24-7."

She turned to the blonde bombshell next. "Mica—you have to maintain the Sharp account. If we lose his business because we're playing do-si-do with Lucius, we can't pay the bills; and that means Lucius wins anyway."

Next, she barked: "Claire—I need 110% of you parked in front of your computer screens, doing what you do best as we plan our attack."

Pete leaned closer to Drake, whispering, "Did she just use a country dance analogy?"

Drake shook his head to shut Pete up.

"Max..." Claire began.

She ignored the interruption. "...*and* I need to know someone has eyes on you at all times."

Claire pursed her lips.

Orders given and received, Maxine clapped her hands, rousing the team to their feet. "Everyone pack up and give me a minute alone with Drake."

Claire slid out of her chair and stormed to her room. As the kitchen and living room cleared, even Pete took his cue and left. Ryan was the only person who remained—and Maxine seemed okay with him lingering.

She turned to Drake and demanded: "Are you up for this?"

"Yes, ma'am."

"It's going to get ugly. Uglier than it has already."

"I won't let them get their hands on Claire again."

"She's going to resist."

"She's pretty much resisted me from the beginning," Drake snorted. "I'll work with her—I won't force anything. As long as the order comes from you, dealing with Claire is up to me." Drake surprised himself with both his words and his conviction. Five minutes earlier, he'd thought he'd be packing and leaving. Now, he was part of the team.

Maxine's eyes narrowed, and she warned, "This job doesn't end until Lucius is behind bars—or dead. I'm not terribly picky which at this point. In any case, his elimination might take weeks, or months."

"I can manage that." Drake had enough in his savings account that he could afford to take time off from his acting career and keep a watchful eye on Claire. He had a few commercials he'd signed on to do, but since those were audio only, he could deliver on them remotely.

Maxine extended a hand. Drake gripped it firmly, but without aggression. She shook hands with him, and then turned and left with her signature abruptness.

Drake scratched the back of his head. "She's quite the leader." He turned to Ryan, who'd been silently watching their interaction.

"If Maxine could pull off that level of intensity on-screen, she'd be the next Meryl Streep or Sigourney Weaver."

"She's remarkable," Ryan agreed. He crossed his arms and gave Drake a level gaze. "She also neglected to mention the consequences if you fail."

Drake met Ryan's gaze. "I believe the threat upon my life was clearly implied—but, by all means, feel free to spell it out for me."

Ryan smirked, and then grinned. "No need to spell it out—not so long as you know."

He left the kitchen.

Alone, and suddenly needing a distraction from the stress of what he'd just signed up for, Drake turned toward the sink and started washing the dishes.

MAXINE FINISHED PACKING and dropped her duffle bag at the front door.

Outside, Drake sat in his Explorer—waiting on Claire as she packed the last of her things and spoke with Mica. Reece had already left, driving a blindfolded Pete back to the airport.

Ryan approached the head of Rider SI. "You're sure about Drake?"

Maxine was glad Ryan had stuck around to question her. She didn't mind a different point of view—she just didn't want the entire group to share their points of view, all at once and in front of Drake.

She turned and looked into Ryan's dark brown eyes. The former Ranger had taken a chance on her and her company by signing on with them, and he'd helped make Rider SI a success. Professional, reliable, and level-headed, Ryan was her preferred counsel on tough jobs. Maxine didn't see as much of him these days—not now he was married—but the trade off in his happiness seemed worth it.

"I'm sure about Drake," Maxine nodded.

"What makes you sure of him? This could all be an act."

Maxine smiled. "Walsh, if it's one thing my bleeding heart, military men have taught me, it's the power of love when it comes to protecting a woman—and vice versa."

Ryan's brow furrowed. "Love?"

"Yep."

"You think Drake's in love with Claire?" Ryan's nostrils flared.

"Yep. It might have started out as an assignment, but there's real emotion involved now."

"How can you tell?"

Ryan possessed exceptionally good skills when it came to reading body language and interpreting expression—but only when he was clear-headed. Maxine knew his anger at Drake for endangering Claire had blunted Ryan's normally sharp powers of perception.

"I can tell the same way I knew you'd found someone special when you came back from Antigua," Maxine met his gaze. "I could tell the same way I knew Mason was falling for Aurora. It's in the eyes and mannerisms."

"Does Claire love him back?"

Maxine shook her head. "I don't know. I'm not sure she can after being lied to."

Ryan snorted. "That's a good thing. She doesn't need to fall for someone like that."

Maxine cocked her head to one side. "Someone like what? Someone who'd risk his own life to save hers? Or someone who made a terrible mistake and wants to rectify it?"

Ryan grinned, dimples emerging above his square jawline.

"Okay—point taken." He leaned in. "How closely do I need to watch them?"

"Your main role is getting them to the Rider office safely, and then checking on them frequently. Security is state of the art there. Claire can board Bear in the exercise room. He'll need walks, and I don't want Claire outside and exposed, which means Drake will be doing the dog walking. They might need you or Mica to make the occasional food run, but otherwise the office has water, a shower, and some pull-out beds."

"What are you going to do?"

"Talk to our allies."

Ryan's eyes flashed. "You mean Comrade Pronin? Speaking of 'it's in the eyes and mannerisms'."

Maxine's face hardened momentarily. She'd stopped making a concerted effort to hide her relationship with Vladimir Pronin, but she certainly hadn't advertised it, either.

"What gave it away?"

"He came to my wedding to see you, Max. You danced with him."

She ran a hand though her hair. "Yeah, I did."

"Besides, you know David and Jenna work at the same hospital now. He's ER, she's ICU. They talk. David mentioned Vladimir."

Maxine's son and Ryan's wife were both physicians. It made sense that whatever David knew would soon become common knowledge with the rest of her team.

"David thought you seemed happy with him."

The conversation had turned uncomfortably personal, but Maxine hadn't spoken to anyone about Vladimir yet—and perhaps she needed to.

"Walsh." Her mouth felt suddenly dry. "I... I'm in *love* with him. It's illogical, and irrational, and probably my downfall..."

"For how long?"

Maxine looked back up. "I don't know. Probably since your wedding. I don't know how to end it. I've tried pushing him away, but he's relentless—and I always end up caving in."

She pointed a finger at her chest. "*I* cave in—and I can't afford to be weak to someone like..." Her voice trailed off.

"Someone like *what*?" Ryan's eyebrows raised. "Someone who'd risk his life to save yours? Or someone who's made mistakes and wants to rectify them?"

Maxine chuckled—both infuriated and impressed by Ryan reciting her own words back to her "Touché."

"He's a man in love, too, Max," Ryan reassured her. "He wants to rectify his past. He's looking to you for how to do that."

Annoying tears welled in Maxine's eyes. Having Ryan Walsh give her understanding, perhaps even permission to give her relationship with Vladimir a chance for success, felt liberating.

Ryan wrapped his big arms around her and squeezed. "It's okay for you to find love, too, Max. Follow your heart. I'd even understand if you two ran away together—like a couple of 55-year old teenagers."

Maxine wiped at her eyes and stepped back. "I have a company to run."

"Do you?"

She stared up at him.

"You know any of us would take the lead if you needed to chase your own happily-ever-after."

"What about Mica?" Maxine asked.

"Ah! So, you *have* considered it." Ryan nodded "Yes, I think Mica's a fine choice to run Rider SI. She's young, but she won everyone's loyalty by protecting David and taking down AJ."

Maxine let out a breath. "Okay. I can't take any more sentimental moments for today. Get your butt on duty, soldier—we'll talk more later."

"Yes, ma'am."

9

———

Claire looked up from packing as Mica entered her room.

"I like the new color. Very chic."

"Thanks." Claire smoothed a hand down her dark bob.

"You want to talk about what happened?"

What *had* happened?

Screaming. Fear. Agonizing paralysis as electricity seared through every nerve-ending in Claire's body—and that had been *before* waking up in a remote torture chamber, left to wait for something gruesome to begin.

Claire shuddered. "I'm just glad it's over."

Mica sat on the edge of the bed. Claire knew she was being studied. She didn't want to look at Mica out of fear that she'd find pity in her friend's expression.

Claire had no desire to be pitied.

Sensing defeat, Mica asked, "What *do* you want to talk about?"

Claire forced herself to grin. "How about your wedding?"

"Um..."

"You still haven't picked a venue, have you?"

"I know I want geraniums," Mica offered. "That's a start."

"You need a destination."

"I don't need anything fancy."

"Yes, you do. You're David's Princess in Shining Armor—and he's your Prince Charming in a white coat. Your love deserves a celebration as beautiful as it is."

"Wow—you're quite the romantic. You should write for Hallmark."

Claire swatted Mica in the arm. "I love happy love stories, that's all. I won't even start reading a book or watching a TV show unless I have it on good authority that it has a happily-ever-after."

Mica arched an eyebrow. "That's not the way the real world usually works."

"Exactly. I live and breathe in the real world. I don't need more of the *real world*." She smiled at Mica. "Did Max ever tell you how she and I met?"

"She did—but I'd like to hear your version."

Claire sat down on the floor, leaning against one wall. She crossed her legs. "I got into MIT. They have this program to evaluate kids in poverty—diamonds in the rough. My high school counselor set me up to talk with a former MIT grad who'd looked at my grades and aptitude tests. She coached me on how to complete my application and essay." Claire stopped to chuckle. "The first line of my college essay began with: 'I grew up learning how to take care of my crack cocaine-addicted mom.' Talk about eye-catching."

She shifted her weight. "Anyway, I got in. That was my ticket to freedom. I wouldn't have to be defined by the roach-infested home

I lived in anymore, or the sketchy neighborhood where women didn't walk alone after dark—or by the parent who never attended a single award ceremony."

Mica slid down to sit on the floor opposite Claire, with her back against the bed. She silently listened to every word.

Claire frowned. "...but I blew it. Fifteen months into college, I got stupid. A friend from high school called me. She was enrolled at this community college, and one of her teachers had made a move on her. She refused to go to the police because she didn't have any proof. Consequently, she dropped the class—but she was worried about how to prevent somebody becoming her teacher's next victim." Claire closed her eyes. "I knew I could help."

She took a deep breath before continuing. "So, I hacked her professor's computer and checked out all of his Internet traffic. Turned out the creep was also into child pornography. At that point, I had evidence. I could have turned it all over to the police —but I wanted to catch more and bigger predators. I wanted to take down all the scum like him. So, I created my own child porn dot-com website. There were no real pictures—just suggestive partial photos which, when clicked, would take the pervert to an 'under construction' page. But after visiting and clicking that site, a virus would be planted on their computers. This virus would track the users' logins to other sites and collect their usernames and passwords."

She raised her hands. "*Et voila!* I suddenly had the bank log-in information of all these sickos. Unbeknownst to them, they began making monthly donations to charity organizations."

"So," Mica mused, "rather than sending one man to jail, you funneled the dollars of dozens of predators to charity? You thought it was better than some old pervert rotting in jail, leaving his money untouched?"

"The donations totaled about $1.5 million—until I got caught. When they found out, I was arrested. I pled guilty. The charge was a first-degree Class B felony, and I was facing jail time. Thankfully, the judge was lenient. She gave me a hefty fine, a year of community service, and a year without the use of a computer." She sighed. "MIT expelled me."

"What about the men and the pornography?"

"I had all of their names and IP addresses because they'd visited my fake website—but my site didn't have any *actual* pornography on it, so the FBI couldn't use the information to arrest them. I don't know that they ever launched their own investigation."

"Damn—so those bastards they got away with it? They're *still* getting away with it?"

Claire gave a devious grin. "Not entirely. For those who were married, I emailed their wives proof of their husbands' indiscretions—along with the number of the FBI hotline to report them." Claire shrugged. "Hopefully, at least some of the wives turned their criminal spouse into the authorities."

She looked up at Mica.

"For those of them who weren't married, I emailed their bosses. Those who weren't married or employed got an email to their mothers."

Mica barked out a laugh.

Claire smiled, but added, "Unfortunately, I was now *without* a college degree and *with* a criminal record."

"But Max found you?"

"She did. She'd apparently heard about my fiasco and had been impressed. She asked if I'd be willing to pick up where I left off—to continue my computer crimes, but do it to help good people. In fact, most of what I do for Max *isn't* illegal—and those whose computer records I *do* illegally tamper with are in no position to report my activity. They'd risk investigation."

Claire looked across at her friend. "So, yeah," she smiled sadly. "I know what the real world is like, Mica. That's why I rule my fairy kingdom, and I fight in my virtual reality games, and I dress up for Comic Con. That's *also* why I want to bask in the sunshine of my friend's happiness when she marries the man of her dreams."

Mica matched Claire's smile.

"Mason and Aurora got married at a California vineyard. Ryan and Jenna were wed at her parent's island resort in Antigua. What location defines you and David?"

Mica turned the question back around. "What would *you* do?"

"Where would *I* get married?"

"Yeah."

Claire didn't even hesitate. "A castle."

"A castle?"

"Yes. There's this gorgeous castle in North Carolina called Smithmore Castle. It's white with picturesque turrets."

"You want a fairytale? Or a wedding?" Mica grinned.

"Both," Claire answered dreamily.

Mica shook her head with a chuckle. Claire knew they complemented each other—both searching for what they'd been denied growing up. Mica had been raised as a tomboy by a military father, who cherished her but hadn't let her explore her femininity and capacity to care for others. Claire had dreamed of escaping inner city poverty into a world of fantasy and fairytales. Working with Rider SI was the chance for both of them to live these dreams.

As comfortable silence fell across them, Claire pushed herself up and off the wall, rising to her feet. "The two aren't mutually exclusive," she sighed. "I can have both a fairytale *and* a wedding —when I get married. But we were talking about your *real* wedding, not my imaginary one."

DRAKE DROVE Claire south on Highway 19. The quiet rumble of the engine seemed to stretch the miles between them.

Reece had driven a blindfolded Pete back to the airport earlier. Drake had apologized to his friend—again—but Pete had been more than happy to return home, where the most dangerous event was a power outage interrupting his game of Destiny.

Now, it was just Drake, Claire, and Bear in his Explorer.

"This is the first time we've been alone since..." His voice trailed off. He didn't want to stir dissension between them by uttering the word 'kidnapping'.

How could Drake repair what he'd done in the past without making things worse by reminding her of it? Why did he even care? Yesterday, he'd been ready to pack his bags and take the next flight back to the California coast. Today, he was on an assignment to keep Claire safe.

She turned to him as he drove. "Since when? Since you rescued me? Are you waiting for me to fall at your feet in gratitude?"

"I *was* going to say since our fight," Drake backtracked. "Since you found out I was working for Titan."

"So it is." Claire stared out the window, her body language closed off. Her black bob covered part of her face—that beautiful face, with its smooth skin and soft, pink lips.

"What I said in Lucius's cabin," Drake gulped dryly. "I hope you know what I said was me acting."

Claire turned to look at him.

He pressed on, "I don't think you're a blue-haired freak, Claire. I think you're beautiful—blue-haired, black-haired, or pink-haired."

"Guess that made me an easy mark," she returned coldly. "Or, it made your decision to make an assignment out of me easier."

Drake clenched his teeth. Nothing about Claire *or* his assignment had been easy, but he didn't think telling her would improve the situation.

"Listen," he tried to explain, "I took the assignment because I wanted real-life experience working for a private security company. I wanted to enhance my abilities as an actor."

"Kudos," she scoffed. "Your acting was superb. I actually believed you *liked* me."

Drake gripped the wheel tighter. "I did like you. I mean, I *do* like you. I'd already made the decision to tell you the truth *because* I liked you—and once my eyes had been opened to Titan's corruption, I truly intended to tell you the truth." He paused. "I just hadn't figured out how to, yet."

"A shocking revelation," Claire deadpanned.

Drake released out a slow breath, reminding himself that Claire had every right to be angry with him. He wished she'd at least acknowledge he was *trying* to make amends.

"Titan took me off you as an assignment right before AJ's arrest," Drake explained. "AJ apparently wasn't happy with my progress—or my lack of it."

The actual discussion had been somewhat more crass—about how Drake hadn't gotten Claire into bed yet. That had never been an explicit part of his assignment, and by the time Drake had realized sleeping with Claire was a heavily implied part of his assignment, he'd already drawn a line in the sand that he wasn't going to cross. He wouldn't sleep with Claire merely as a way to get information for Titan Enterprises.

"I was demoted back to escort duties," Drake told her, "which was fine. I'd already decided I had no interest in uncovering any secrets about you or your company, or handing them over to Titan."

He sighed. "Anyway, I was driving Chong in a limo around town..."

"Fo Chong?" Claire interrupted, turning to him sharply. "He's the head of Chinese crime in Atlanta!"

"Yes, I know that—*now*. Anyway, he got tipsy—so my working day morphed into an evening party. The party included heroin and hookers—at least one of whom I'm pretty sure was underage."

"And you didn't call the police?"

"That's a decision which can't be made lightly," Drake snapped defensively. He slowed the pace of his words—anxious to explain a complex situation that Claire seemed keen to oversimplify.

"Titan Enterprises is made up of former military and police. Everyone who works there has something to hide—that much I figured out after my first two weeks. Everyone also has connections to law enforcement. It's a network buddy system—so if somebody reports to the wrong person at the precinct, *they're* the ones who'd find themselves with a one-way ticket across the river Styx." He shuddered. "Lucius's men are all *more* than happy to tell you about the whistleblowers whose employment—and lives— were prematurely ended after they'd tried to report things to the authorities. Those deaths were all accidents, of course—nothing that could be traced back to Lucius."

As Claire stared at him, Drake responded, "I've got photos of that night with Chong—but I haven't been keen on turning them in and shortening my life expectancy."

He waited for Claire's next jab, but it didn't come.

Instead, she picked at her blue jeans. Her voice drained of all hostility and judgment when she murmured, "I know Max assigned you to protect me, but you could be so much more."

Drake glanced in the rearview mirror—checking to confirm that Ryan was still following along behind them.

"More?"

"Yes," Claire nodded. "You know all about Lucius's inner organization. You could help us take him down."

The idea appealed to Drake on many levels. First and foremost, he wanted to help eliminate the threat that Lucius posed to Claire. Next, Drake had his own desire for revenge—one that had burned ever since Titan's employees had hurt Claire and drugged her dog. Finally, Drake also felt manipulated by the company—but, then again, he'd faked his identity to join them, so perhaps that one was his own fault.

There were other reasons Titan Enterprises needed to be brought down. There were the drugs and human trafficking, which Drake had been ill-equipped and lacked the resources to fight against alone...

...but with the resources of the Rider SI team, they might just...

"...*but*," Claire interrupted his thoughts, "it's dangerous." Her tone sounded cautionary rather than baiting.

"I'm pretty sure rescuing you already put me on Lucius's shit-list," Drake snorted. "Lucius knows I'm aware of at least *some* of his dirty deeds, so the target's already been painted on my back—to use Maxine's words." He glanced over at Claire. "So, yes—I'd like to help."

Claire gave Drake a slight smile, which lifted his heart. Although it was small and fleeting, she hadn't given him a smile since she'd discovered the Titan Enterprises business card in his wallet, back what seemed like a lifetime ago now.

Drake turned his attention back to the road. He didn't want to read too much into Claire's expression. She'd naturally be grateful for anything he could do to help Rider SI—her team and her family—defeat Lucius Titan, so Claire's smile wasn't necessarily indicative of her forgiveness.

WHEN MAXINE ARRIVED BACK in her neighborhood, she took precautionary measures. She drove past her house first, checking for anything suspicious or out of the ordinary. She spotted no cars, no surveillance, and nothing that suggested anything sinister.

After she'd parked in her driveway, Maxine circled the outside perimeter of her house. She saw no signs of forced entry and no trampling of the flowerbeds beneath the windows. She finally decided it was safe to go to her front door.

Maxine punched in the security code and stepped inside her house. She tugged off her jacket and hung it on the coat rack secured to the wall, kicking off her boots.

A deep voice suddenly emerged from the kitchen: "Do you care to tell me why you're sneaking around your own home like a burglar?"

Maxine, already on edge, immediately started reaching for her gun—until she recognized the deep timbre of Vladimir's voice. She breathed a sigh of relief, smiling at the irony of being relieved to see the leader of the Russian Mafia waiting for her in her home.

"I didn't see your rental car," Max said, stepping into the kitchen, "so I thought you were out."

Vladimir stood in the kitchen in blue jeans and a white, button-down shirt. By the smell of Italian herbs permeating the house, he'd been cooking.

"Boris needed to borrow it," he explained. "Why the cloak and dagger routine?"

"Claire was kidnapped. She's safe now—but Lucius has officially transformed from a pain in the ass to a real threat."

"Kidnapped?" Vladimir voice was a snarl.

Maxine startled. Was he angry with *her*?

"She's safe now."

"Kidnapped!" Vladimir's face turned as red as a radish—the muscles in his neck straining with fury. A small vein bulged on his forehead.

Maxine knew that rage. She'd felt it herself, when she'd first realized that Claire had gone missing. But Claire wasn't part of

Vladimir's team. She wasn't part of *his* family—so, what had caused the big Russian to become so angry?

"What's wrong with you?" Maxine demanded.

"What's wrong with *me*?" Vladimir stormed over to her, physically pinning Maxine to one wall with his large frame. His hands rested on either side of her.

She scowled at him. Although Vladimir's anger was palpable, she wasn't afraid of him. He'd been a Russian soldier, hardened by the harshness of border patrol before he'd become the ruthless leader of the Russian mob. He'd killed men and ordered the execution of many more. Yet, despite his violent past, Maxine didn't fear him. If she did, she wouldn't have given him the code to her house.

She didn't fear Vladimir Pronin—and she certainly wasn't going to cower from the temper tantrum he was now indulging in. Maxine tried to shove him off, but he didn't budge. "What's gotten into you?" she hissed.

Vladimir's breathing was heavy. "*Chert poberi*! You disappear overnight, and I give you space, because I respect that you're a busy woman. Then, you tell me one of your team members was in danger? When were you going to involve *me*?"

He was so close she could *feel* his deep, Russian-accented baritone as much as hear it. Maxine started to open her mouth, but then faltered as she realized the source of his fury. He was angry at having been excluded.

She hadn't intentionally left Vladimir out of this. She'd just been alone so long, it hadn't occurred to her to include him when disaster struck.

"We're supposed to be a team, Max," he growled.

They *were* a team. She and Vladimir had worked successfully together on several operations—mostly against Lucius Titan. So, why hadn't she included Vladimir this time?

Habit. She'd run Rider SI alone ever since she'd started the company.

So, Maxine understood the source of Vladimir's anger—but she still wouldn't be bullied by him. She narrowed her eyes at the Russian. She was a Marine. She didn't have to explain her actions to anyone, least of all...

Vladimir's firm body pressed against hers, and Maxine suddenly realized that his panting was no longer due to anger.

She bunched his shirt in her hands and bit her lip.

Vladimir's gaze turned smoky as he growled her name. He still wanted his answer—but she had other plans.

Maxine pulled him toward her and met no resistance. They kissed—and the contact grew more heated as Maxine lost herself in Vladimir's rugged strength. How could this man be both ruthless and compassionate? How could he be both complex and simple? How could Vladimir Pronin make her go crazy with lust when she hadn't felt this way about anyone in decades?

Before she realized it, they'd made their way to the bedroom and were lying horizontal on the bed together. Clothes were discarded, and Maxine lost herself in the heat of the moment.

10

———

*L*ater, as they lay side-by-side on the bed, spent and catching their breath, Maxine placed a hand on Vladimir's chest.

"I should have told you. *Ya proshu proshcheniya*," she apologized.

"We're a team?" Vladimir rolled onto his side to look at her.

"We're a team," she agreed. Maxine didn't know where this relationship was going—where *could* it go? But she knew they were a team.

"Claire is okay, *da*?"

"Yes. Oddly enough, her boyfriend rescued her."

"She has a *paren*?"

"Sort of."

"If you had told me about the abduction, I could have assembled a team."

"I *have* a team—and we're good at what we do. We would have cased the area and led a stealthy offense."

"Heat signatures? Silencers? Tear gas?"

"We didn't have enough time for all of that." Maxine flopped back on the pillow, staring at the ceiling.

"Two hours and I could have dropped a team by chopper to rescue Claire."

"You could do that in two hours?"

"Probably less. My position has its perks."

She turned to look at Vladimir—this man whose affections and resources she routinely underestimated.

"I can eliminate Lucius Titan for you, too. Would you like me to count the ways?" He lifted her hand to his lips and kissed the back of it.

Maxine chuckled. "As romantic as that sounds, I have my own score to settle with Lucius. We've been building toward a battle for some time now—and I don't want him dead." She paused. "Well, I *do*—but I've vowed not to succumb to that part of my past. The part where it's easier to pull a trigger than hold someone accountable."

"You want him in an American prison?" Vladimir's tone sounded bored. "You think the punishment fits the crime?"

"No—but it never will. If it ever did, then the justice system would have become no better than the criminals."

Vladimir's intense eyes watched her. "Why don't you tell me all the sordid details about this nemesis of yours?"

Maxine rolled out of bed. As appealing as lingering in bed with Vladimir sounded, they had work to do. As she dressed, she told Vladimir the story. "I learned about Lucius Titan when I was stationed in Helmad Province. I was a staff sergeant E-6. There was a cluster of insurgents near Washir, but they were wolves among sheep—hiding within a group of villagers. Men, women, and children. We couldn't go in—not Marines, not Rangers, not Delta Force. The civilian casualties would be too high."

Vladimir kept his eyes on Maxine as he pulled on his jeans. Once dressed, he followed her into the kitchen.

"Generals above my pay grade made a decision to hire a private security team," Maxine continued. "Not Titan Enterprises—Lucius's company wasn't created yet—but the organization was named Blue Peak, and Lucius worked for them. He led the expedition outside Washir. Codename: Phoenix."

Maxine poured two cups of coffee. Vladimir stirred the marinara sauce he'd left simmering on the stove. Maxine leaned against the counter, staring into the black void of her coffee cup as if it were a gateway to her past.

"My team reached the area first after their massacre. It was sickening."

Silence filled the room for several heartbeats. The sound of the humming gas stove and sizzle of sauce were the only noise.

"'The evil men do lives after them'," Vladimir quoted.

Maxine looked up and blinked at him.

"Shakespeare," he explained.

"Perhaps a statement which could be made about any of us."

Vladimir took his hands in hers. "Some of us learn from our evil deeds and make course corrections. Lucius chooses not to."

She looked at their entwined hands, and then up at him.

"I have my sources, too," Vladimir murmured. "Lucius has no boundaries. There's no limit to who he'll steal from, kidnap, or murder." Vladimir gave a chuckle at her expression. "I see what dances behind those blue eyes, Max. You're wondering how I am any different."

The big Russian sighed. "I *do* have limits, and there *is* honor among thieves." He shook his head. "*Naprimer*, take Lucius's trafficking of women. I don't buy or sell women. Some women choose to sell themselves—their bodies—but I have no problem with that. Some would prefer earning three thousand rubles an hour by having sex than three hundred peeling potatoes. Their decision is the fault of a broken government, not the Russian Mafia. We merely step in and play the middleman. We get paid a cut, and in return the women don't have to negotiate a price, deal with a nonpaying customer, or be taken advantage of. It's safer and cleaner."

Vladimir rolled his shoulders. "I try to tell the—what do you call them? *Sutener...*"

"Pimps."

"...*pimps*," he nodded, "to treat those women like their sister. There are repercussions for forcing such women into anything. Obviously, Sonya, Mikhail, and I—we can only take action on the infractions we know about." He sighed. "Anyway—my point is that I *do* have standards. Lucius doesn't."

"I would never compare you to him."

Everything about Lucius Titan—from his motives to his methods—was slimy and tainted.

Maxine squeezed Vladimir's hands in reciprocation of his affection.

Vladimir had shown himself to be a man capable of immense change. His brutal life on border patrol, and a series of early tragedies, had led him to seek the strength only organized crime could provide amid the chaos of Communist Russia. That life had made him hard, and he wasn't proud of many things he'd done to rise in the ranks of the Russian Mafia—only some of which he'd shared with her.

"You'll include me on everything from now on, *lyubov moya*?" Vladimir's deep voice always warmed Maxine when he called her '*my love.*'

"Yes." She set down her mug and turned fully toward him. "Starting with the Cronus Protocol."

The Cronus Protocol was named for the Greek Titan.

If Maxine planned to take down a Titan, she needed a worthy plan. The Cronus Protocol was a scheme that she and Vladimir had brainstormed for the inevitable day when she'd need to unleash it upon Lucius Titan.

That day had come.

Vladimir arched his eyebrow as he regarded Maxine. "Okay," he snorted. "I still think the name is—how do you say? *Over the top*? But we'll get it started."

CLAIRE WALKED INTO THE BUILDING—HOME of the Rider SI offices —with Drake and Bear in tow. She intentionally walked fast, avoiding eye contact with Drake. He might be assigned to her— but protecting her in no way required constant verbal communication.

Besides, what was Maxine playing at by even involving Drake in this mess?

Claire repeatedly pressed the button to summon the elevator, knowing it wouldn't come any faster the harder she pressed. While she appreciated Drake's willingness to help, aiding the Rider team only made him more of a target.

Claire had already seen him get shot once. He'd be safer back in California. Drake wasn't qualified to be a protection detail.

On that note, images of him fighting in the cabin suddenly flashed before Claire's eyes. Okay, she admitted—maybe he possessed *some* of the necessary qualifications. Plus, it seemed like he had his own axe to grind with Lucius Titan.

But in that regard, Drake would have to get in line. Everyone at Rider SI had a reason to want Lucius behind bars—or worse. Ryan had seen the man's devious deeds firsthand, when Lucius had killed one of his friends. Mica had been manipulated by Lucius and AJ to find someone they wanted dead. Mica had thought she was bringing someone in to be arrested for a bounty—instead, she was inadvertently aiding a planned hit job.

Vladimir wanted Lucius dead, too—because Lucius had helped an Argentinian drug dealer orchestrate a contract hit on Vladimir. Thanks to Maxine, it had failed—and Maxine had subsequently kept Vladimir from eliminating Lucius with his own resources.

Lucius Titan was a deadly, dangerous man. Did Drake have any idea how risky this mission was? Then, she remembered how he'd been shot while attempting to rescue her.

Okay—so maybe he *did* understand how dangerous this was; and yet Drake had still chosen to protect her.

She was running out of reasons to dismiss him. But what if the next time Drake got shot, he wasn't wearing an insulated electronic device for protection?

Claire needed to get a vest on him. Back at the cabin, when she'd thought he'd been shot and killed, she'd...

Claire cringed inside. Even the memory of it stole her breath.

As the elevator rose, she looked down to see she'd reflexively taken hold of Drake's hand. Angrily, Claire shook her hand free and side-stepped further away from him.

"Sorry."

"I didn't mind." Drake's deep, smooth voice hummed through her.

The enticing tone of his voice was one of his many infuriatingly attractive features. Drake even made part of his living doing voice overs for commercials and recorded introductions to TV show trailers, and she suspected he was good at it.

When the elevator finally arrived on the third floor, Claire walked hastily to the offices of Rider Security and Investigation. She entered a key code on the door behind the reception desk.

"Welcome to Rider Security and Investigation," the hologram

behind the desk greeted them. "Please sign in on the electronic tablet."

"That's cool," Drake murmured, as Claire led him past the flickering projection of a woman standing behind the desk.

She ignored his awed expression. "First, we'll get you outfitted."

Claire led Drake to the equipment room, unlocking it with another electronic key code.

"Whoa!"

The walls divided the room into three sections—one for handguns, one for other hand-held weapons, and one for bullet-resistant vests and gadgets. Claire pulled a vest off the wall and thrust it at Drake.

"These generally work better than electronic tablets."

He took the vest, but his eyes stayed wide as they roamed the room.

She walked to the gun rack and pulled down a handgun. "This is…"

"…a Sig Sauer P229. Holds 13 rounds. Semiautomatic, with no safety." When he caught her surprise gape, Drake said, "I know guns, Claire."

He took the weapon and checked the chamber.

"Good," she grudgingly responded. "Ammunition is in the drawer. I've got work to do."

Claire stomped from the equipment room. She needed to distance herself from Drake—both him, and the urge to crawl into his arms to feel how alive they both were after facing down death at that remote cabin.

She felt Drake's eyes watching her walking away.

"Okay. I'm here if you need anything."

She left him in the equipment room—feeling like she'd left a kid in a candy store. Since the room contained nothing explosive, she hadn't left him in any danger.

Claire entered her office, flicking on the lights and powering up her hard drive and all three monitors. She had a mound of work to do in preparation of an offense against Lucius Titan. The attack would require an infinitely longer period to plan it than actually execute it—and it would require her to be on the top of her covert, computer-spying game.

First, Claire needed to perform a comprehensive review of all the personnel files of Titan employees. She needed detailed schematics of his office and business holdings. She would also have to scour all the financial information they had on Lucius—both public, and not-so-public—and find weaknesses and discrepancies to exploit.

Three months' worth of work needed to be done in a week.

But Claire loved a challenge. She stretched her torso, flexed her fingers, and sat down to work.

⁂

RYAN TAPPED on Claire's shoulder, and she jumped, pulling the ear pod out of her ear.

"Sorry, didn't mean to scare you."

Claire's black hair accentuated her big, brilliant eyes and gave her a more mature appearance. She'd covered part of the bruise on her face with makeup, but Claire still looked beaten and tired.

The tiredness came partly from having worked three hours non-stop. Ryan had run into Drake on his way in, and Drake had told him how focused Claire had been on this assignment. He'd been in the kitchen area, where he'd had hot water simmering for Claire's next cup of tea.

Claire smiled. "Hey, Ryan."

He leaned against the doorway. "Take a break?"

He held out the cup of tea Drake had prepared for her.

Claire stood, stretched, and took the tea. "Thanks. Where's Drake?" She tried and failed to keep her tone casual.

"Walking Bear."

"Oh, good." Her dog needed the exercise.

Claire wriggled the tea bag in the steaming water, not making eye contact with Ryan as he stood in the doorway.

"How's Jenna?" She eventually asked.

"Jenna's well." Ryan had called Jenna as soon as they'd secured Claire at the safe house. He'd given her an update on the situation, urging Jenna to take the precautions he'd taught her to stay safe.

In a few hours, he'd go home and be with her.

Claire nodded. She brushed past him, out of her office, and they began walking down the hallway together.

Ryan wondered how many thousands of times Claire had walked and paced this office hallway. Ride SI was her home away from home.

Well, currently it was just home.

Ryan suspected conversation might help Claire take a reprieve from work.

"Jenna's actually great," he told her. "Cal will be visiting for spring break next month, so she's looking forward to seeing him. This summer, we'll be scoping out colleges. Jenna's hoping Cal will choose Emory or UGA, but there's no skiing close by."

Jenna's son, Cal, attended a boarding school for competitive skiers.

"You like being a stepdad?"

Ryan loved Cal. They could horse around like buddies—and Cal was good to his mother, which earned him son-of-the-year award in Ryan's book.

"Cal's cool. Jenna had me give him driving lessons leading up to getting his license. I took him off-road with one of Mica's dad's junkers last time he visited and taught him some getaway driving techniques."

"I'm sure Jenna loved *that*." Claire gave a playful roll of her eyes.

"She's actually very supportive of Cal learning self-preservation—probably since she herself was kidnapped."

They reached Maxine's office. There, Claire picked up the photo of Ryan and Jenna from the desk. It showed them together on the beach in Antigua, on the afternoon of their wedding. The framed picture beside it showed Mica and David hugging beneath mistletoe. Another photo was of Mason and Aurora. Mason's wife was all long legs in her blue, formal gown, while he wore a tuxedo. The photo was from a fundraiser they'd attended. The trio of photos brimmed with bliss and love.

On one wall, Mica's wedding dress hung, wrapped in protective, transparent vinyl. Ryan watched Claire gazing at it. She'd helped Mica find it, and they'd decided to keep it at the office where David couldn't see it.

"We're just one big family, aren't we?" Claire touched a hand to the dress.

"We are," Ryan nodded, "and you've been like a younger sister ever since we met. Family looks after each other, Claire." He took the photo and set it back on the desk. "Maxine and Mica assured me you're doing okay—but recovery from a kidnapping is a process."

"I was only kidnapped for a few hours." Claire bobbed her teabag in the mug.

He turned her chin toward him. "You were still forcefully abducted and held against your will, Claire..."

"...*and* I watched Drake get shot."

"So I heard."

"He was wearing his friend's jacket," Claire said quietly. "It had his electronic tablet in an inside front pocket. The bullet hit the tablet." Her voice trembled slightly. She had researched such an occurrence online—tablets weren't bullet proof. Drake had been damn lucky. Since the bullet was a .22 and the tablet also had a hard rubber case, he'd been left with a nasty bruise but no permanent damage.

"Drake's fortunate to be alive." Ryan pulled her into a hug. "So are you."

Big brother, little sister. That's what it felt like.

He smiled as he remembered the first time he and Claire had hugged. They'd just finished a harrowing rescue, during which Claire had navigated them to safety. When the Rider team had been reunited, Claire had hugged Ryan with delight that he was safe—at the same time making the observation that he felt like big, firm teddy bear to her.

A teddy bear! Ryan had killed men—but Claire had hugged him and referred to him as a stuffed animal. He couldn't help but laugh.

"I still can't believe Drake managed to rescue me."

"Maxine told me she'd instructed him to wait, but Drake was worried that the interrogator would arrive before the Rider team could get assembled."

"I'm glad he didn't wait." Claire stepped back with a shudder.

Ryan appraised her, trying to make his own determination as to whether Claire was emotionally stable after all she'd been through. The prospect of an interrogation wasn't a laughing matter—and Claire wouldn't be able to make that trauma disappear as easily as she changed her hair color.

He crossed his arms. "So, is black the new blue?"

Claire ran a hand through her sleek hair.

"Well, black is the new *me*." She threw him a smile. "Don't worry. My office fairy lights are *not* coming down."

"Good. Don't change too much—we all love your quirks."

Bear suddenly lumbered into Maxine's office and nuzzled his nose into Claire's hand.

Ryan turned to see Drake standing in the doorway. He gave Claire a winning smile, which made her cheeks flush crimson.

Well, Max was clearly right about those two.

"Can I get you anything?" Drake asked.

"I'm good. Just taking a break."

He nodded, and then nodded at Ryan before walking away down the hall.

Ryan and Claire watched as her dog followed Drake of his own volition.

11

Drake slipped his Bluetooth earpiece in while he ran on the treadmill in the workout room of Rider SI.

Like Claire, he couldn't risk going home and being targeted by Lucius. The ruthless man still wanted information from Claire—but Drake felt certain that the only thing Lucius would want from him was his quick and convenient death. Drake knew he'd be killed without hesitation simply for his involvement—or rather, his interference—with Claire's kidnapping.

Even as little as walking the dog outside this building posed a hazard to Drake's health—and required him to wear a bullet resistant vest.

It occurred to Drake that the last two days were just the sort of role research he thought he'd wanted when he applied at Titan Enterprises.

Now, such aspirations seemed foolish in the context of all the danger he'd submerged himself into: First with Titan, and now at Rider SI.

The danger he was part of. The danger enveloping Claire.

Drake finally knew true terror—after having stared down the barrel of that gun just before being shot back at the cabin. It left a large nasty bruise that would be tender for day, but it could have been much worse.

The Bluetooth earpiece buzzed as Pete answered his phone.

"Hello?"

"Hey, Pete. Drake here."

"Ah, still living and breathing, I see. Rescue any more damsels in distress?"

"Very funny. I wanted to make sure you got home okay—and to apologize. I'm sorry I involved you." Drake kept a steady pace on the treadmill, which allowed him to evenly breathe as he jogged.

"No worries, man. Now that I'm home safe, I can look back on it with pride instead of paralyzing fear. I told my RPG buddies I'm the man who *unleashed the hound!*"

Drake chuckled. "Yeah, you are."

"How's Claire?"

"In the zone. She's scouring every aspect of Lucius's life. He doesn't stand a chance."

"When are you coming back to LA?"

"I guess when this is over." Drake wasn't in a hurry to leave Claire, but he also wasn't one to linger where his presence wasn't desired. He was only staying now because Maxine had dictated it. He assumed that when the CEO of Rider SI had no further use for him, neither would Claire.

The earpiece buzzed again as Drake received a text message.

"Got to go."

He hung up on Pete and read the text.

It was from Catherine: *I heard what happened. I guess we're finished.*

Drake typed a reply: *No, I'm working on another plan.*

Catherine responded: *Forget about it. Forget about me.*

Drake: *I won't break my promise. We just need to find another way. I'll be in touch.*

He returned his phone to his pocket.

He hoped Catherine wouldn't give up on him. She was just one more reason he needed to stay in Atlanta a little longer. Claire's kidnapping had meant the plan he and Catherine had devised was no longer feasible. He'd have to find another way to help her.

MICA MET Mason at a coffee shop across the street from Bill Sharp's office building.

Since he was tall, with blond hair, blue eyes, and a body sculpted by the rigorous exercise routine engrained in him from his Navy SEAL training, the women in the coffee shop all turned to watch Mason stroll in.

He noted their gapes the way anyone in the security business stayed attuned to his surroundings—but he didn't meet the gaze of any of the women or invite their eyes to linger. He kept his wedding ring in plain sight.

Mica looked at the titanium band on Mason's left index finger. She needed to pick rings out for her and David. In fact, she needed to do a lot of preparations for their wedding, since, so far, she'd only gotten as far as buying a gown.

"Thanks for coming," Mica said.

Mason sat across from her. "Sure thing, boss. I *can* call you boss, right? It feels like we've been making a transition from Max to you recently."

They *were* transitioning ownership—in practice, even if not yet on paper.

Maxine had broached the topic with Mica only two weeks ago, as something the CEO of Rider SI wanted to test out—slowly delegating more and more leadership responsibility to Mica to see what reaction the team had.

So far, Maxine's employees—who knew of the change—had accepted it without complaint. Mica knew there'd be bumps in the road, but if anyone had concerns, they hadn't expressed them yet.

Perhaps they were saving them until they'd finally dealt with Titan.

As for Mason? Mica smiled. "I'm okay with boss. What do you call Max?"

"Max, or boss, or ma'am."

Mica wrinkled her nose at the last word. "I'll take Mica, or boss. You and I are the same age, so ma'am just feels weird."

"Okay." Mason looked at the tabletop, and his eyes fell toward her coffee cup. "Do you read?"

She arched an eyebrow. "You mean for pleasure?"

"Yeah."

"Sometimes. Plane rides usually."

"What genre?"

"Thrillers."

Mason nodded with a wistful grin. "Max reads romance novels. I think I'm going to miss the meet ups when I catch her carrying around a book about cowboys or billionaires."

Mica chuckled. She hadn't seen Maxine reading any romance novels since she'd met her several months ago, and she wondered if that was because Maxine had unwittingly secured her very own billionaire. "I wonder if she'll still read them in retirement."

Mason shrugged. "How's Dorian?"

"Perfect for the part. How's Aurora?"

"Bowing out of the tour."

"Oh, no. Is she injured again?" Mica asked.

Aurora had suffered an ankle injury years ago and been forced to fight her way back into the top ranks. That wasn't the reason, though.

Mason grinned. "We're expecting."

Mica beamed. "That's fantastic!"

His voice dropped lower. "We haven't made a big announcement. We want to wait until Lucius is out of commission."

Mica wondered if the delay was so everyone would be free to rejoice—or whether it was so Lucius wouldn't make a target of Mason's wife and unborn child.

Of all the Rider team, Mason and Aurora had never directly offended Lucius; but their association still put them both at risk.

"I understand," Mica nodded, "and it should only be a week. Maybe two."

They wouldn't fail. Couldn't fail.

So much was riding on the success of eliminating Lucius Titan.

"What do you have for me now that the missing persons case is solved?" Mason asked

"There's a gala," Mica nodded. "Max and several of us need an invitation. It's an exclusive fundraiser for rainforest preservation. Attendees will mostly be rich and famous—senators, movie stars, Fortune 500 CEOs..."

"...and Lucius Titan?"

"And Lucius Titan," Mica confirmed. "I thought Aurora might have connections."

Mason leaned back. "If she doesn't, her parents will."

Aurora Meridian's parents were California wine tycoons. Mica hadn't met them yet, and she'd only met the tall, blonde, athletic

Aurora once before, over the holidays, but they still felt like family to her.

The Rider team might be small—especially in comparison to Titan Enterprises—but they all had connections; both to each other, and to the kinds of people who could help them get their mission accomplished.

"Is it smart to go after Lucius at a such a high-profile party?" Mason's tone sounded curious, rather than skeptical.

"This won't be the grand finale," Mica reassured him. "This will just be a warning shot across the Titan bow."

Mason's brow furrowed. "Is that supposed to make things better, or worse?"

"He kidnapped Claire and would've tortured her," Mica shot back. "It's hard to even imagine worse. Anyway, Max wants to confront Lucius—a face-to-face encounter will enable her to demonstrate her conviction, and give her an opportunity to assess his."

"And this staring contest will take place at a high-profile fundraiser, where security will be everywhere—so no one can get an itchy trigger finger."

"Exactly." Mica sipped her coffee.

"So, does Lucius knows about this planned rendezvous?" Mason asked.

"No—and we need to keep the element of surprise. I'll give you the aliases to use on the guest list to get us in."

"Consider it done."

"Thanks, Mason."

Mica stood, but Mason held up his hand. He smiled at her.

"Listen, Mica. Whatever southern breeze you brought with you when you joined this team and reunited Max with her son—it's been a pleasant one. Max has her son back, and she's happy. Russian mobster aside, I think her mood has a lot to do with you and David."

"Thanks."

"We're glad you're here."

———

LUCIUS TITAN CLICKED to advance the slideshow displayed on the screen that dominated one wall of his enormous office.

"As you can see, Senator, our security is top of the line—both nationally and internationally. We've protected politicians, celebrities, and America's top 1%." He leaned toward his potential new client. "We've even done overseas operations that were a little too dark for the US Military—but obviously, I can't discuss those."

He rocked back on his heels with a wink and a smile. "We can certainly manage your security detail with precision, sir."

The white-haired Senator looked contemplative, but appropriately impressed by the Titan Enterprises presentation—but wasn't leaping to sign on the dotted line.

Lucius understood the politician's dilemma. He wanted the highest-level of protection for his family and himself—but the hefty cost was cause for pause.

You have to pay to get the best.

Despite the hesitation, Lucius could tell that the senator was leaning toward accepting Titan's expensive services.

Lucius's phone buzzed to life. He retrieved it from his suit coat pocket. "Excuse me, Senator. Please, take your time with the packet and the estimations of cost and delivery I've given you."

As he stepped into an adjacent room, Lucius closed the door behind him and answered the call. "You have something?"

Faint screaming, as if through a closed door, transmitted through the phone.

"He's a bit cantankerous." The gravelly voice on the other end of the line belonged to one of Lucius's contractors—a man who'd been dubbed Truth Serum. "He's screaming bloody murder, but he still hasn't told us where the weapons are hidden."

Lucius scratched his chin. "You've done electric shock?"

"Yeah."

"Skin peeling?"

"Arms and legs."

"Genitals?"

"Mutilated."

Lucius shrugged. "Okay. I guess he really doesn't know. Put him out of his misery and get rid of the body."

"Okay. What about his wife?"

Lucius gave a *tsk*. He'd almost forgotten he'd had his men kidnap the FBI agent's wife as well. There were so many exhausting details to juggle in this job.

Currently, he was focused on his recent clash with Maxine Rider and the tedious planning of her demise—but, in the meantime, all the other aspects of Lucius's business still needed to continue. For example, he needed to find a hidden weapons stash for one client, and also turn this Senator into another paying client.

"Threaten her life in front of him. If he doesn't talk then, he really doesn't know anything."

"And if he *doesn't* know anything?"

Lucius waved a hand in the air dismissively as he talked, even though Truth Serum couldn't see the gesture. "Kill them both. Get rid of the bodies."

"Okay—and if he *does* know something?"

"Verify it. Eyes on the payload before you dispose of them—but *then* dispose of them." Lucius hung up the phone and dropped it back into his pocket.

After straightening his tie, he plastered on a winning smile and rejoined the Senator in his office. "Do you have any questions?"

DRAKE WALKED to the receptionist desk of the Rider office to meet the delivery boy. When the courier pressed the summons button, Drake made him recite the origin of the delivery: Sharp Industries.

This correlated with the delivery Claire expected from Bill Sharp.

Since being assigned as Claire's protection, Drake was taking every precaution. He wouldn't let any harm come to Claire—not ever again—and he wouldn't let Lucius sneak some type of Trojan horse into Maxine's office, either.

"What's the Doctor's preferred mode of transportation?" Drake asked the courier.

"The TARDIS."

The young man answered blandly, warily eyeing the hologram behind Drake.

Since the courier had given the correct answer, Drake signed for the package. He wondered if the courier got the *Doctor Who* reference, or just mechanically memorized any code words Claire forced him to recite.

Drake watched the courier leave before carrying the box to Claire. The 12"x12" cardboard box wasn't particularly heavy, so Drake wondered which critical component of Claire's scheme was contained within it.

He found Claire in the company gym. She wore yoga pants and a tight-fitting, gray T-shirt. The form-fitting clothes left little to the imagination.

A thin sheen of sweat had formed on Claire's skin from the exertion of her movements. For a moment, Drake stood there and watched Claire's combat moves as she battled a virtual fighter— seen only by her through her headset. Claire's graceful moves looked more like a dance than hand-to-hand combat.

Maybe she'd make a good stunt woman, he mused.

But Drake knew Claire didn't like fighting, and that she was far more valuable to Rider SI—and the world at large—when she was behind the scenes, working her computer magic. Her on-screen talents were in covert operations with a computer, not Hollywood.

He balanced the delivery on one arm and rapped his knuckles against the open door.

Claire pulled off her headset.

"Special delivery."

"Oh! My nanoparticles!" Claire skipped over to Drake and inspected the shipping label.

"Nanoparticles?"

Claire set down her headset and ran her hands over the box—as if it contained the Mona Lisa. Images of Claire running her hands over him in the same manner, not to mention the same rapt attention, suddenly had Drake sucking in his breath.

"Nanoparticles," Claire confirmed, oblivious to how intently he was watching her enthusiasm. "They're smaller than a pinhead and the technological advances are ever-expanding—renewable energy, medical cancer therapies, and so on. Despite their small size, they create a large surface area. They can be bonded to store hydrogen or electricity. Some buildings even use nanostructure with photovoltaics for solar energy to power the offices, or hold heat better. Lucius has his building windows coated with nanoparticles to scramble infrared beams used to measure room vibrations as a surveillance technique."

"Remarkable," Drake wasn't sure how much of that he'd understood. "So, no one can spy on Lucius's office?"

"Right," Claire nodded. "If I had a spare million dollars, we could line the windows at our office with the same." She took the box from Drake and started to walk to another office.

Drake followed. "Why do I sense you're not using these nanoparticles to reduce your carbon footprint through solar powered energy?"

She grinned at him—an endearing and mischievous expression. "No, I'm not."

Claire set the box on a table lined with other boxes. They were now standing in what appeared to be storage room.

Drake glanced at the label. "What does Sharp Industries do?"

"Bill Sharp? Sharp Industries? You've never heard of him?"

"No."

She blinked at him. "He's one of the world's largest weapons manufacturers."

"Why would I know that? I'm an actor, remember?"

Claire opened her mouth... and then closed it again.

Instead, she looked down and picked at one edge of the white packaging label. "Right. I guess I've been getting so accustomed to you being around the last two days, I've started thinking of you as part of the team."

Part of the team.

He wanted Claire to think of him as *more* than part of the team. When she looked up at him through her long, dark lashes, he even dared for the impossible—to perhaps resurrect a romantic relationship with Claire.

But instead of focusing on that, Drake gave her a crooked grin. "Now if you'd said Tony Stark of Stark Industries, I'd know *exactly* who you were referring to..."

Claire chuckled. "Right—an actor needs to know his Marvel characters."

"You and I did see the last *Avengers* movie together."

She cocked her head to one side. "That's right. We did, didn't we?"

Drake watched Claire's eyes twinkle at the memory. He remembered the feel of her soft hand in his during the show. When he'd taken her home, he'd earned a goodnight kiss from those soft, supple lips of hers. Then, she'd had to go inside—

because Bear was barking for attention from her yard, perhaps warning Claire about Drake.

Drake hadn't kept Claire from Bear. He didn't want to find out if her flimsy, white picket fence was sufficient to keep a determined Bullmastiff trapped in her yard.

Now, in the offices of Rider SI rather than in front of Claire's house, Drake leaned closer to Claire with a smile.

When she didn't move away, his heart kicked faster...

...right up until Bear padded into the office, nudging himself firmly into the space between Drake and Claire.

Drake looked down at the intrusive animal. "Guess he's ready for a walk."

Claire rubbed a hand along her dog's head. "I can't believe he trusts you." She looked up. "I mean, I'm glad he does—I'm just surprised."

Drake's phone chimed with a text message, but he didn't pull it out.

"Bear *tolerates* me," he clarified. "It's not as though we're friendly."

Drake had been taking Bear outside for walks three times a day, but the dog still hadn't made any additional effort at bonding.

Then, as if on cue, Bear pushed his head into Drake's hand.

Or maybe he has.

"I'll leave you to your nanoparticles. C'mon boy." Drake and Bear left the room together.

As they reached the lobby, Drake pulled on his vest and jacket and hooked Bear's leash onto his collar. After grabbing a plastic bag, he took the dog outside for a walk.

Drake braced himself for the February chill and light drizzle, which gave the streets, cars, and buildings of Atlanta a glistening sheen.

As he walked, he pulled out his phone to see Catherine's text message.

What news?

Drake texted her: *Retaliation planning is underway.*

Catherine typed back: *How soon???*

Drake responded: *I don't know yet—but we'll get you to safety.*

Drake walked around the block, waiting for a reply. When Catherine didn't send another message, he hoped it wasn't a sign she was giving up on him.

⸺✥⸺

MAXINE AND VLADIMIR sat across each other at the dinner table, eating the chicken Parmesan he'd cooked. He had an affinity for cooking Italian food, and Maxine enjoyed every dish he'd made.

They'd spent busy days apart since Claire's kidnapping—coordinating their independent efforts to mold their grand plan against Lucius.

Researching Lucius from every tedious angle, followed by adding painstaking layers to their surveillance and schemes, had made this operation seem as delicate and intricate as laying pistachios and honey across fragile filo dough to make baklava.

"Can I not convince you that this face-to-face meeting with Lucius is futile?" Vladimir asked as they ate.

"It's part of the game."

"Your game—not his." Vladimir poked a fork in Maxine's direction.

"I want a clean conscience when whatever happens, happens. If I go to this gala and confront him, then I'll know I gave him an out—another option." Maxine drank a sip of her Merlot.

"But you know he won't take it..."

Maxine set down the wine glass and stared at the dark, red liquid. "Do you remember the first time we met?"

"*Da*, of course."

Maxine had arranged a meeting behind the security gates at

the Atlanta airport, so she could discuss one of her clients with Vladimir knowing that neither of them carried any lethal weaponry or surveillance equipment.

At that time, Vladimir's niece had been sending Maxine's client hate mail.

"I didn't think you'd agree to help," Maxine said, remembering the occasion.

"I helped because I have a respectable side, *da*? Lucius does not."

"I concede that point—but I didn't know about you and your honor at the time. It's the same with Lucius. If I don't *try* with Lucius, then I can't really know if he has an honorable side or not—I can only assume. If I *do* confront him, and he behaves in his predictably pompous manner, then my course will remain unaltered, but at least my conscience will be clean."

"I can't talk you out of this? And I can't convince you to let me kill him?"

"No."

"I didn't think so." Vladimir cut into his chicken. "So, I rented a tux."

Maxine looked up sharply. "But I didn't invite you."

"I'm aware."

"Why would you go? You *want* Lucius to know you're helping me?" She took a bite of her broccoli.

"I'm certain—thorough man that Lucius is—that he's already aware of our relationship."

Maxine grunted agreement as she swallowed. "Still—you're spotlighting yourself."

Vladimir cocked his head to one side, eyes sparkling. "Are you worried about me, *dorogoy*?"

She set her fork down and leveled her gaze at him. "I care about you, Vladimir."

He gave her a warm smile. "Well, if you're going to show Lucius a wall of solidarity, I need to be a part of it."

"Okay." She nodded coolly. "As you said before—we're a team. *Komanda.*"

Maxine extended a hand across the table, which Vladimir grasped gently.

He nodded.

12

*L*ucius met his morning client in the foyer of his building, where he could walk him past the blue and gold mosaic tiled fountain and the metal sculpture of a phoenix. The decorative structures gave testament to the financial robustness of Lucius's company.

Lucius extended a hand and smiled. "Lucius Titan."

The tall, lean man shook his hand. "Abdul Patel."

"I hope your travels went smoothly."

"As smoothly as international travel can."

"Your English is quite remarkable." Lucius escorted Abdul to the elevators.

"I studied in England. That was some thirty years ago." Despite the crispness of his words, Abdul still had an accent—

with which the 'th' sounded like 'd' and his voice reached a crescendo at the end of each sentence. "Now," Abdul continued, "my clients are from around the world, so I must be worldly."

"You have an impeccable reputation."

After they entered the elevator, Lucius pressed the button for the fifth floor.

When Abdul Patel had reached out to Lucius with an email, requesting a sizable delivery, Lucius had Hoyle run a background check on him. That revealed the Indian was respected in the underworld community and known for acquiring whatever those with money desired: Stolen works of art, new identities, or—in this instance—women and drugs.

Using Lucius as supplier, Abdul wanted to fulfill a request from Shiv Memon, leader of *Bada Bombay*—Mumbai's second leading organized crime syndicate. Shiv wanted twenty virgins and an assortment of drugs, including a kilogram of heroin, a kilogram of cocaine, ecstasy, and rohypnol. The order needed to be ready in two weeks—when Shiv Memon was due to visit the US. This request marked the largest of its kind Lucius had received, and he was anxious to see if Abdul and his sponsor would be able to cover the sizable cost. Abdul would have to prove that the expenses would be covered by providing half up-front, and half on delivery.

Lucius glanced at Abdul in the reflection of the spotless steel elevator doors. The man possessed a calm composure. He'd already agreed to, and been subjected to, a thorough search—so Lucius knew he was neither armed nor wired.

"You have many cameras in your offices," Abdul noted.

"All closed circuit. Impenetrable."

"All the same—if we reach agreeable terms, the final delivery should be somewhere without so many eyes."

"I can accommodate your request," Lucius nodded.

If this transaction proceeded amicably and the exchange was

made, Lucius might have forged a valuable alliance with Shiv Memon.

⁂

DRAKE RECOGNIZED Lucius's building from across the highway. The exterior was a modern, square structure with windows on all sides. Despite its unassuming appearance, there sat the Devil's lair.

Beside him in the car, Claire wore sunglasses and a baby blue scarf wrapped around her neck, just above the collar of her tan jacket. She looked upward while launching a drone into the sky, expertly operating the handheld control. The whirring drone rose and then hovered above the car.

"They'll notice that thing hovering outside the windows." Drake squinted against the sun, watching the drone moving further away from them and up toward Lucius's building.

"I'm not going near the building," Claire reassured him. "See those telephone poles? I'm going to place the cameras on top of those, so I can watch the building at all times."

Claire expertly piloted the drone until is squared off above the top of a towering telephone pole. There, Claire deployed the camera the drone carried—placing it on the flat surface at the top of the pole with the deft expertise of a world-class pilot.

"Won't it blow away?"

"I put adhesive on the base of the camera." Claire directed the drone back to their car. After it landed, she began to load the next camera onto the bottom of the drone.

Drake watched her focus on her craft. He hadn't seen this intense side of Claire before—not until he'd spent these last few days in the office with her. On their dates, she'd usually been energetic and effervescent—like the way she'd spent Comic Con pingponging from one vendor and display to the next—but Drake decided he liked this added dimension of her personality, too.

One by one, she deployed a total of three cameras—two on top of telephone poles, and one on a large, flat branch of a tree. After she'd finished, Claire packed the drone back into its protective case and stowed it back the Explorer. Then, they sat in Drake's car with the heat cranked all the way up.

Claire stuck her hands in front of the passenger-side vents of the dash. "It's a little chillier today. I think I'm ready for spring."

Drake took her hands in his and massaged them, warming them up in his firm, dry grip.

"Wow. You're better than a heater." She smiled at him. "Thank you."

As Drake held Claire's hands, he held eye contact no less firmly. His mind raced. How could he build a bridge to close this gap between them? Would she even consider dating him again if he asked?

Her wide eyes watched Drake with calm interest. Claire wasn't looking away, and she wasn't withdrawing her hands from his. That was a positive sign, right?

"Claire, I..."

Drake's phone suddenly chimed with a text message.

He reluctantly pulled his hands from hers, pulled the phone out, and glanced down at the interruption.

Catherine had messaged him: *Can you talk?*

"Sorry," he told Claire, as he stared at the screen.

He texted Catherine back: *No. Are you okay?*

Catherine responded: *Yes. Just wanting to know what the plan is.*

He replied: *Soon.*

"Do you need to take that?" Claire asked.

Drake had held his phone at an angle, so she couldn't see the screen.

"No." He tried to sound nonchalant as he put the phone back into his pocket.

· · ·

CLAIRE SAT in silence as Drake drove them both back to the Rider offices.

They parked in the garage, walking together to the foyer to take the elevator upstairs.

Claire had sensed Drake that hadn't wanted her to ask him about who he was texting, and she'd wanted to respect his privacy. After all, Drake had demonstrated his dedication—all-in—to the Rider mission. She felt she could trust him.

Mostly.

But Claire hadn't shared the details of Maxine's plan with him, and he knew nothing of the Cronus Protocol—other than its name. This wasn't because of mistrust, though. That decision had been made as a form of protection—just in case Lucius abducted Drake and used the man they called Truth Serum to extract that information from him.

Drake seemed to understand this—and he hadn't pushed Claire for more information about the Rider team's offensive plans.

Claire reached her office, shrugged off her jacket and scarf, and sat down at her computer. Drake stood over her shoulder, watching as she logged into her computer. The cameras she'd placed with those drones came on-line. Claire focused the different views.

She smiled as she looked over her shoulder at him—proud of her handiwork.

"Three views of his building—parking, entrance, and exit. The only thing I can't see is if someone bails out a window on my blind side—but I doubt that's a very likely scenario."

Drake's gaze scanned the video images. "You're brilliant."

She stared at the building for a moment—the building of her nemesis—and a shudder ran through her as she recalled the grim cabin she'd been held captive in.

"You okay?" Drake asked.

Claire swiveled around to look at him. Drake's chestnut hair—longer on top—had fallen slightly across his face as he'd leaned over. He'd grown a few days stubble. There was a small line between his brows, and Claire wondered if that line had formed from filming countless scenes of smolderingly intense, on-screen expression.

Was she okay? Claire honestly didn't know the answer to his question. As long as she kept herself busy all day, she didn't have time to think about how she felt. She still hadn't taken the time to process the kidnapping.

"Let's take the rest of the day off," Drake suggested. "I'll pick up lunch, and we'll share some wine."

An hour later, they'd eaten lunch and were sat on a sofa in one of the conference rooms. Drake had pointed out that there was large monitor—which they could have watched a movie on—hung up in the other conference room. That room only had a conference table in it, though, rather than the couch they were currently enjoying.

"It's clearly backward," he teased.

"It's meant for business," Claire countered. "Maxine never designed the offices thinking her employees would be living here. Besides, this is a nice ambience for conversation."

The room they were currently in had a smaller screen on the wall, plus the couch, in addition to two large, cushioned chairs. A plush, golden shag rug lay in the middle of the room, and Bear had claimed it as his own.

Drake reached over and pulled Claire's feet into his lap.

"Okay, so let's converse.'"

The relaxed gesture surprised her, and she was even more surprised when he started massaging her aching feet.

"Is this okay?" he asked.

"It feels divine." She took a sip of her wine. "So, tell me something quirky about Drake Fitzgerald—something I don't know about you. I know you're a stunt double and you do voice commercials and voice-overs. I know you like football…"

"Go Rams."

"…*and* you're not afraid to fight."

Drake laughed. "I *was* afraid. I was actually more terrified than I'd ever been in my life that day in the cabin—but I was more fearful of what they planned to do to you, rather than anything that might happen to me."

For a moment, Claire felt only his soothing hands on her feet and heard the deep, relaxed breathing of her dog.

"If you hadn't gotten there when you had…" She hesitated, thinking of the stench of Jerry's body odor and her kidnapper's hungry, predatory eyes. Then, she sighed deeply. "I suppose I *should* talk about it." She felt as if she was telling herself this as much as Drake. "If I don't get it out, it'll just fester inside me."

The lump of fear she'd carried with her ever since her kidnapping had started to feel exactly like that—like a festering boil in need of lancing and draining.

Claire took a deep breath, before continuing: "Someone on Lucius's payroll was coming to torture me. He'd been flown in from somewhere and was on his way to the cabin right when you arrived."

"I know all about him," Drake said gently.

Tears welled in Claire's eyes. "…but before he got there, Jerry said he planned to… He was going to…"

"I know," Drake said softly. "I know what kind of scumbag he is."

Claire felt something in her chest start to ease—as if it was cracking, and giving way. It was as if she'd been wearing a tightly laced corset ever since the kidnapping and was only now blissfully free of the crushing pressure.

Drake leaned over and gently pulled her into his arms. They

lay on the couch together, and as she lay her head on his chest, she felt the rise and fall of Drake's breath.

"I guess one quirk about me is that I'm a huge Greek mythology fan," he began. "I'll read any books that have something to do with Greek mythology—old or new. From *The Odyssey* to *Circe*. I read the entire *Percy Jackson* series to my nephew over the course of a summer. Needless to say, I was stoked to hear you had something called the Cronus Protocol to use against Lucius."

Drake shook his head, laughing. "I even chose to work for *Titan* Enterprises partly because of the name."

"You went to work for Lucius because of his *name*?"

"Partly—and partly because I didn't want to find myself protecting a fellow actor or anyone else in the acting industry I might know. I figured the opposite coast was a safe bet."

Claire snorted. "Well, I don't know much about Greek mythology, but even I know the Titans were bad news."

"I guess the name should have warned me off." He lazily stroked a hand through her hair.

"Do you have a favorite Greek character? Odysseus perhaps?"

"No. Smart though he was, I don't agree with some of his life choices."

"A favorite god then?"

"They were all cruel."

"A demigod?"

"Perseus," Drake said. "He rescued his future bride and stayed virtuous to her."

"Nothing says chivalry like beheading Medusa."

When Drake chuckled, Claire felt the pleasant rumble through his chest.

"You *do* know some Greek mythology," Drake said.

"I learned Perseus from *Clash of the Titans*," Claire explained.

"Ah, I see."

She craned her neck and looked up at him. "I'm going to call it a night early." She pushed herself up from Drake and stood. "Can you stay with me? Maybe just snuggle?"

Did Drake snuggle? Would he be completely put-off by the term? Would he read something deeper into the request, other than just a prolonged embrace?

"I'd love to hold you, Claire—for as long as you'd like."

RYAN WATCHED Hoyle eating dinner with two of Lucius's other men at a barbecue shack.

"Surveillance, surveillance, surveillance," Reece groaned. "When do we get to fight?"

"You complain—but when we fight, it creates paperwork, and then you complain about that."

Reece shrugged as he adjusted his position in the passenger seat. Their vehicle was parked right on the curb. "But then, you do the paperwork for me—so it's all good."

Ryan grunted. "What I'd prefer is to be at home with my wife."

"At least this mission is in Atlanta. You still get to see Jenna every day."

"True." It was true, but because this battle was on their home turf, it also meant everybody's loved ones could be in danger.

Ryan kept no secrets from Jenna. His wife knew what the Rider team faced in their clash with Lucius. In fact, Jenna was one of the reasons Ryan was keen on taking down Lucius. The head of Titan Enterprises had a reputation for hurting the loved ones of his enemies—and Lucius could decide at any moment to retaliate against any of the family members of the Rider team. In fact, he'd already gone after Maxine's son, David, through the actions of AJ, last year. Ryan couldn't stomach the thought of anything happening to Jenna—especially not as a result of his entanglement with Lucius.

"When this is over, do you reckon Maxine and Vladimir will ride off into the sunset?" Reece twirled one end of his mustache.

"I hope so. I'd like to see her find happiness."

"He's certainly an interesting choice of significant other, though."

"A man with a checkered past? Who tries to rectify things he's done when he can?" Ryan shrugged. "I can sympathize. After all, Jenna loves me despite the person I once was."

Ryan could have made a move against Lucius during his own employment there. *Could* have. If he had, he might be a dead man right now—like his friend Jeremiah. Yet the lack of action felt more like cowardice some days, rather than logical self-preservation.

Ryan turned to Reece to alter the conversation a touch. "God only knows what Jess sees in *you*—but she hasn't left yet."

"She's left many times," Reece pointed out.

"You know what I mean. She moved from Chicago with Jenna partly because of you, and she's still in Atlanta. She hasn't given up on you."

"Well, aren't you the optimist?"

"You two are compatible."

"You make us sound like Tupperware. Besides, we fight whenever we're together." Reece crossed his arms. "Of course, the makin' up is nice."

Ryan chuckled. "She's good for you, Reece—and if you called more often and sent flowers occasionally, you might even fight less. She's the type of woman who doesn't waste her breath on people she doesn't want to associate with. If she's fighting with you, it's because she thinks you're worth the fight."

The corner of Reece's mouth curved upward as Ryan's words resonated with him. "Weren't we taking about Maxine?"

"Yes—and I think she'll do okay with Vladimir, but he's going to have to climb down from his leadership position in the Russian

Mafia to do it. He's already begun handing over power to his niece."

"Still, it's not like it's an elected position—from which he can just gracefully step down from the podium and relinquish to somebody else. The man's got enemies. Those enemies might become Maxine's enemies if she stays with him."

"Agreed. They need some type of anonymity."

Through the window of the restaurant they were watching, Ryan suddenly saw Hoyle stand and shake hands with the other men he'd been dining with.

"They're wrapping up." Ryan started the vehicle's engine.

"Oh, good. Maybe he'll stop for ice cream next." Reece sighed and pulled on his seatbelt.

MICA SAT with Claire at a coffee shop as they waited for their rendezvous. Two tables away, Ryan Walsh sat drinking coffee and reading a newspaper.

Mica watched Claire, who was watching the door. Her friend appeared anxious, but not beyond the normal, buoyant energy Claire was usually possessed by. Everyone at Rider SI worried to what extent Claire would suffer post-traumatic stress from her kidnapping. Mica and Maxine had reminded Ryan, Reece, and Barry that Claire might dress like an enchanted fairy refugee—but she'd grown up knowing the harshness of reality. Despite her up-until-recently blue hair, she was a smart, resilient woman.

"How's Drake?" Mica asked.

Claire turned from the door to her friend. "Protective, attentive, compassionate—And, of course, he's gorgeous. It's hard to stay angry at a caring, attractive man."

"Maybe you don't *have* to stay angry."

Claire narrowed her eyes at Mica.

She shrugged. "Come on—I think the rest of us forgave Drake the moment he accepted Maxine's assignment to protect you, without hesitation."

"We snuggled," Claire said.

"As in...?"

"As in sleeping in his arms all night long—it was wonderful." She turned the paper cup in small circles on the tabletop.

Claire turned her gaze back to the entrance of the coffee shop as Special Agent Eddie Finch entered the cafe. He wore a blue suit, and his hair was crested in a high wave above his forehead. The federal agent pulled off his sunglasses and nodded at Mica.

"You dated *that* guy?" Claire asked in a harsh whisper. "He's so GQ and full of himself."

"Yeah, well," Mica turned her eyes away from Claire. "He was a big shot FBI agent, and I wanted to be just like him."

"Good thing you didn't turn out that way."

"Yes, it is."

Eddie unbuttoned his jacket and sat in the empty chair at their table. "Mica," he greeted her with a smile. "You must be Claire."

"Claire Maltisse."

They shook hands.

"Yes, I checked your background, Claire. Kicked out of MIT for illegal computer hacking." His tone held the distaste of someone in law enforcement addressing a criminal.

A defensive flare surged through Mica on behalf of her friend —one that had Mica wanting to snap Eddie's two-hundred-dollar sunglasses in half.

"I turned everything over to the FBI," Claire responded coolly, apparently unfazed by Eddie's condescension.

"The report *did* say you provided full cooperation." He gave a grim, pursed lip expression. "I assume I'm here today because you've once again uncovered something—and now you plan to fully cooperate with yet another investigation into something you *illegally* found out."

Claire grinned.

Eddie had agreed to meet with them because Mica had hinted she might hand him another career-defining arrest—just like she had when they'd brought down AJ. The Rider team had orchestrated AJ's captivity by providing incriminating evidence, and then let Eddie swoop in and lay claim to all their groundwork.

Mica leaned back and crossed her legs. "We're still gathering information at this stage."

"Information about who?" Eddie tapped his index finger against his sunglasses as they rested on the tabletop.

"Lucius Titan."

Eddie's brow furrowed. "The private security specialist? AJ Schlau's boss? Who claimed to know nothing of his employee's indiscretions? We've subpoenaed files, but nothing incriminates Titan—and he protects a *lot* of wealthy and influential people. We already took heat anytime we got near him."

"It's a good thing you don't mind taking the heat, then—not if it means bagging a bad guy," Mica countered.

Eddie was a dependable, by-the-book agent—which also meant he abhorred people who got away with dirty deeds because of their political connections. The slight grin on his lips indicated to Mica that her flattery was working.

Claire shifted in her chair. "We'll get incriminating evidence on Lucius."

Eddie turned to look at Claire. "If you get it illegally, it's of no use to me."

"We'll ensure we provide the information in a form that you can use," Claire said.

"When?"

"It's still a work in progress," Mica said.

Eddie nodded, and then stood. "You know how to reach me—

and you know I can only accept this if we keep the FBI clean. I don't want a bunch of evidence which will get thrown out of court once the defense team look at it."

Mica nodded. "Of course." Standing, she added, "Listen, Eddie—I was sorry to hear about Perry Carson." She'd learned of the FBI agent's death in the news.

Eddie's expression turned pained. "Tortured to death—him and his wife."

"Any suspects?"

"No."

13

ucius strolled through Centennial Olympic Park with Hoyle beside him. Lucius needed to stretch his legs, away from the office, and had chosen to grab some fresh air. Since he hadn't managed to eliminate Claire Maltisse, he was aware that she could be remotely spying on him from the Rider SI offices—even at this very moment.

Lucius needed an update on the status of his own surveillance of the Rider team. He knew Claire was holed up in Maxine's offices. That building was a block from a police station and had a virtually impenetrable security system, so Lucius had left her alone—for now. His plan to cripple the rest of Rider SI would decimate the company, and Claire would be out of a job soon anyway.

"Where are we with keeping tabs on everyone?"

Hoyle wore jeans and a brown, leather jacket. "Ryan and Reece are done. We're tracking their cell phones. As for Mica—we've got an insider on Sharp's team who knows her and Bill's whereabouts at all time. As for Maxine—we're tracking her Crossover."

"What about eyes or ears in her building?"

"No—but we were able to access the conference server they use, so the next time they do a group conference call, we can listen in."

"Good. What about the strike teams?" Lucius adjusted the collar of his peacoat more snuggly around his neck before tucking his hands back into his pockets.

"We've got a solid plan for Ryan and Reece. They visit a specific bar every week, predictable as clockwork. Mica will be targeted when she's with Sharp, so the hit will look like it was on him—not her. He has a lot more enemies."

"And Maxine?"

"Trickier—especially since you'd said you wanted her and the Russian mobster taken out together. I'm still sorting out the details there."

"Okay. We'll keep eaves dropping until an opportunity presents itself. Switch gears and give me an update on Abdul Patel."

"He checks out," Hoyle said. "I spoke directly with Shiv Memon, who confirmed that Abdul is representing his interests. Also, Abdul's got older contacts on the black market, who are willing to vouch for him. He's been the middleman for everything from drugs, to women, to art, to hits -for-hire. Seems he's good at delivering *and* keeping his hands clean."

"How so?" Lucius stopped by the large, Olympic rings.

"Occasionally, his clients have been busted—but his record has stayed squeaky clean."

Lucius smirked. He could say the same for himself. As long as he kept people like AJ or Hoyle in the trenches, Lucius was able to keep his own documented efforts—meetings, invoices, and travel—on the legitimate side of his business, so he'd never be caught out. Lucius respected Patel's methods. He admired such forethought in a business partner.

"Arrange the exchanges," he told Hoyle.

MICA CURLED into David and ran a hand along his bare chest.

"Are you still feeling feisty?" David asked.

"I just never get tired of touching you."

He reciprocated with a warm hand along her neck, curling his fingers into her hair. "I never tire of anything you do while naked."

She stroked the stubble on his jaw before running a hand through his brown hair. "Claire thinks we should get married in a castle."

"As long as I'm not required to wear hose, or a kilt, or pointed shoes." His green eyes twinkled.

Mica laughed. "None of those—though you in a tux would be delicious."

"You saw me in a tuxedo on our first date."

"Yes, but we were rudely interrupted by the Sunset Sliders." AJ Schlau had hired a hit on Mica and David, and they'd barely escaped with their lives.

"I remember seeing you vault over the balcony railing in your evening gown. It was just one of the many times you've taken my breath away."

"Well, bullets flying through the air tend to make people breathless."

"I assure you—it was your grace and beauty, not the bullets." Mica grinned.

"Speaking of bullets, how is Claire holding up?" David asked.

Mica always told David everything about Rider SI. They had no secrets.

"She's good. We met with Eddie Finch today. We needed to get his buy-in for when we take down Lucius."

"I'm sure Agent Finch will agree to anything which earns him extra kudos while not having to get his hands—or that suit—dirty."

"You're not wrong." Mica rolled onto her back and stared up at the ceiling. She sighed. "We need to cripple Lucius, David. A simple arrest is insufficient. We need to impact his entire infrastructure."

"Things have escalated with him, haven't they?"

"His fatal mistake was kidnapping Claire."

"Fatal?"

"Fatal to his company."

"I know you, and Maxine, and Claire are all smarter than that monster—but he's more ruthless."

Lucius will come for each of us, Mica thought. David was right to be concerned. The Rider team's best defense was a good offense.

"Please be careful," David added. "You know I support what you do—I *love* that you protect people—but you still have to come home to me. Every night. That's nonnegotiable." David ran a hand between her breasts and down her bare abdomen.

Mica sucked in a ragged breath. "Well, you're my Prince Charming. There's no place I'd rather come home to."

David rolled on top of Mica, pressing his bare skin against hers. He kissed her—deep, sensuous, and passionate.

"I'll say our vows wherever you want me to marry you, Mica. I'm yours forever."

———

MAXINE ENTERED her office and punched the key code. She hadn't been back here since Claire's kidnapping. She'd been working on her plan against Lucius with Vladimir—including the Cronus Protocol, among other details.

As she walked past the hologram, she thought about what retirement meant—a hard earned rest for her weary bones and some sort of freedom to pursue her relationship with Vladimir. She could relax and enjoy the deep-seated happiness she felt in being around him. She'd been burying those feelings up until now —beneath some misguided superstition that acknowledging her attachment made it something she was more likely to lose. Everything she'd valued in life, she always slowly lost—her first husband, who'd fallen out of love with her. Her son, although she'd gained him back. Even her physical prowess had been lost during her Marine days, during a helicopter jump. She flexed her ever-aching knee.

Yet, Vladimir wouldn't leave her. He maintained enough stubbornness to put up with her—and also enough cleverness to stay alive amid the treachery of the world. So, she'd eventually acknowledged her feelings for him—and now even dared to formulate a new life with him.

Drake appeared, coming down the hallway toward her. He looked rested compared to the first time she'd seen him, right after the kidnapping. Drake wore slacks, a button-down shirt, and had a gun secured in a shoulder holster.

"Maxine," he beamed.

"Well—you could pass as one of us."

Her compliment made his bright, white smile widen.

Except you're too damn pretty.

Drake would need disguises for any spy work, but he could still perform security details, like those Barry and Billy were assigned to. Then, she stopped herself. What was she even thinking? Drake was an actor—not ex-military.

And yet, he'd had enough brains and skill to rescue Claire, all by himself. His demonstration that day had been better than any interview Maxine could have conducted.

Bear padded down the hallway too, and stood beside Drake with his tongue lolling out, before finally lumbering over to Maxine and sniffing her—his acknowledgement of her presence. She gave the dog a pat on the head, and after receiving it, he turned and bumbled back to stand beside Drake.

"How's Claire?" Maxine asked.

"She's good. She's intensely focused on everything Lucius-related. I think she misses walking Bear."

"She's in her office?"

"Yeah. I'll give you two some space." He walked away and turned toward the gym, with Bear following his every step.

As Maxine knocked on Claire's partially open office door, she nudged it open with her knuckles. She smiled at the familiar scene—Claire seated before three 24-inch computer monitors with her earbuds in and her head bobbing lightly to inaudible music. The fragrance of lotus petals and amber filled the room from a nearby, scented candle. Above and around Claire, her strings of golden LED lights gave the office an enchanted glow.

An ache settled in Maxine's chest. She'd miss this when she retired. While Claire remained oblivious to her presence—not having heard the knock over the music from her earbuds—Maxine pulled out her phone and took a picture. She captured the computer genius in her magic lair—fairy lights and all.

"Claire." Only after Maxine had pocketed her phone in her cargo pants pocket did she tap on Claire's shoulder.

Claire turned, smiled, and took out her earbuds. "Max!"

Maxine wouldn't be able to capture the jubilant greetings Claire always gave her on a phone—but she was planning on retiring, not exiling herself completely. She'd still see Claire. In fact, she'd still see all of the Rider team—only less frequently.

"Status check," Maxine demanded.

Claire stood and stretched. "Everything seems to be lining up. I've got detailed schematics of all of Lucius's holdings. I've collected a profile on all his employees—well, all the ones I know about through Ryan and Drake, plus anyone I see walk into the building."

Claire the clairvoyant, Maxine mused. Claire might not have extrasensory perception, but she could gain information about anyone almost as if she did.

"What about Dorian?"

"Cronus Protocol is full-speed ahead. Dorian sends me encrypted messages, so I know we're working synchronously."

"Good—and Drake?"

Claire stuck her hands in the pocket of her jeans. "He's good. He's doing a good job. He's taken stock of all our supplies and does regular perimeter checks while walking Bear. Drake's a little stir crazy cooped up in here, I think—but he's taking the role seriously."

"The two of you are getting along?"

Claire's cheeks flushed pink as she scuffed her foot along the carpeted floor. Maxine pursed her lips. Claire had no poker face.

"Yeah. We're good."

Maxine shook her head.

"What?"

"As long as you're happy, Claire. That's all I care about. I'll be in my office working for the next hour if you need anything. Next is the gala, then our conference call. After that, you won't see me until all this is over."

THE NIGHT AT THE GALA, Claire wore a satin, navy-blue cocktail dress and heels. Looking around the room full of the rich and famous—only a few of whom she'd heard of—she felt wildly out of place.

Music from a live quartet filled the room. Champagne flutes danced around the room—transferred from the trays of waiters to the manicured hands of the exclusive guests, and then back to the trays again once they were empty.

The computer operator knew she had no business being there. If only this was Comic Con and she was in costume again. Here, at a gala, she felt naked and exposed.

An imposter.

Drake placed a warm hand on the small of Claire's back. He whispered reassuringly in her ear. "You look amazing. You're the most beautiful woman here."

His tone held such absolute conviction that Claire turned to look at him. For a moment, she studied the sincerity in his eyes.

"Dance with me," he said.

Before she could reply, Drake was already leading her to the dance floor—where other couples swayed to the music. His arms wrapped around her, and his body moved so closely to hers that Claire could feel the heat radiating from him. He looked debonair in his tuxedo—like James Bond. It was ironic that out of all the spies and agents she worked with, the one who currently most looked the part was merely an actor in a role.

She swayed with him, apologizing, "I don't really dance."

Drake smiled. "You're doing fantastically. Besides, I've seen your virtual fighting. You're very graceful."

Claire swallowed. "What are we doing Drake?"

"We're backing up Maxine as she confronts Lucius," he stated simply.

"That's not what I mean." Claire knew why they were attending the gala together, but not why they were on the dance floor.

In fact, Claire understood very little about what was

happening to her right now. She knew who *she* was—just a girl from the ghetto, with a mother who'd sold her body for cocaine. Claire wasn't even a college graduate. She was just a computer hacker, who certainly didn't belong at fancy fundraisers like this one. She was a free, yet broken spirit—and a poseur if she thought she could find happiness in the arms of a movie star.

"We're dancing, Claire," Drake explained, pressing his body closer as he spoke—as if sensing Claire's discomfort with the ambience. "I'm dancing with a beautiful woman—and right now, I feel like the luckiest man here. As if I'm holding Princess Andromeda in my arms."

She looked into his clear eyes, wondering if his words were sincere. Drake sounded genuine—but how could that be possible?

"I'm not one of you," she sighed. "I don't belong here."

Drake cocked his head to one side, regarding her carefully.

"You think your past excludes you from the crowd? Just because they look glamorous, carry lofty titles, and wear shiny bling? Let me let you in on a little secret, Claire. By your criteria, everyone here is some type of imposter. No one is righteous. Everyone hides things about themselves."

He looked around and gave examples, without identifying the specific people to whom those examples might relate. "There's the senator's wife who's addicted to oxycodone, or the actress who started her career with porn—but now fights the stigma of women being reduced to sex symbols. There's the CEO who donates millions to charity, while simultaneously bribing the woman he had an affair with into silence. Nobody here is genuine. You don't get to be here by being genuine."

He turned back to meet Claire's eyes.

"It's the same way with poverty. The gangster who shoots a rival gang member, before going home to change his mother's adult diapers because she's debilitated after a stroke. There's the cop who jails murderers to protect his community—but takes bribes to let drug dealers go free because he's got college tuition to cover for his kids." He paused, leaning closer—giving an example that made Claire shiver: "Then, there's the little girl living in fear, raising herself in grim reality, but never abandoning her dreams and fairytales."

Claire felt her cheeks burn pink.

Drake's lips curled, and he held her tightly in his arms as they swayed to the music.

"Every one of us is a walking tower of complex contradictions, Claire. Nobody has life figured out. There's no magic formula." He leaned closer and placed a kiss on her cheek, before whispering into Claire's ear, "The real reason you belong here at this gala with these people—each with their own faults and insecurities—is because you *are* here. You deserve an amazing event as much as anyone else here does—and you deserve to enjoy it."

"Wow. That felt inspirational." She laughed nervously to deflect from the intensity of her feelings. "Those could be lines in your next movie."

Listening to them, though, Claire had straightened her spine —so she was now standing taller, unburdened by the emotional weight his words had effortlessly hoisted from her shoulders. She kept her body close to his, savoring the way Drake's breath on her neck felt, sending tingling arousal down the length of her spine.

Drake gave her a lopsided grin. "You inspire me, Claire."

She smiled in return, gazing into his bright eyes.

"I do have to ask about this strategy though," Drake asked, breaking the moment.

"What about it?"

"We're here confronting Lucius, right? It seems obvious that if we can achieve this, we can get to him. Why aren't we already taking him down?"

"We have to have proof of his criminal activity," Claire cautioned. "It's not enough just to get up close and personal. We need to catch him with his hand in the cookie jar, so to speak—so there's an ironclad case against him."

"Okay," Drake nodded. "I see your point. I guess I'll let the experts handle it." He paused, smiling softly. "As for the rest of this dance, though—I'll handle that. I'm going to enjoy my time with you while I can."

14

———————

*M*axine scratched her shoulder along the spot where the lace touched her bare skin. Here she was, in another damned dress.

Maxine Rider had spent her decades in the Marines wearing camo and cotton, only occasionally needing her dress blues. Since starting Rider SI, she'd had to wear evening attire multiple times a year. Being an entrepreneur carried a public profile she hadn't considered when she'd launched her business.

Except tonight, Max wasn't here to promote her company. She was here to make a statement on behalf of her employees.

Maxine circled the room with a glass of champagne in one hand. At one end of the ballroom, Claire and Drake danced slowly together. Maxine wondered if the couple's closeness meant she'd be in yet another dress in the near future—this time, for their engagement party or wedding. Then, she corrected herself. Perhaps she was getting a little ahead of things.

Maxine walked leisurely away from the dance floor and around the ornate tables, adorned with their starched, white cloths and matching chairs. The centerpiece on each table was a bold Poinciana, each one a bowl-shaped blossom of vibrant red and orange petals. The tropical flower seemed an appropriate choice for a 'save the rainforest' fundraiser.

Maxine spotted Lucius in a tuxedo, talking to a senator and her husband. Judging by the smiles, Lucius was oozing his typical charm and flattery. She'd heard he possessed those traits, but she'd never seen them being displayed before. She felt as if she was watching a wild animal in its natural habitat—like a monkey in a tree among his social circle, picking lice and preening the others.

Lucius's motives, of course, were to acquire even more lucrative clients. He probably *would* pick lice off somebody if it paid a high enough price. The more she observed Lucius, the more she felt bad for maligning monkeys with her analogy.

Maxine continued to watch Lucius from a distance, until he was finally alone, looking around the room for the next rich and influential person with whom to schmooze. When she approached him, instead, he blinked.

Lucius's surprised expression quickly turned into a smirk. "Maxine Rider? Well, I didn't expect to see you here. I didn't recognize you."

He wouldn't, she thought. Her hair was fixed into a smooth updo, thanks to Mica. She wore a black dress adorned with sequins and lace, paired with short heels and elegant silver earrings. She'd even applied make up for the occasion.

"Lucy," she greeted him.

Lucius's jaw tensed the way it always did when she had the audacity to call him what nobody else dared to.

Lucy.

His voice was cold when he responded, "I didn't think you were particularly worried about protecting the rainforest."

"No more than you," Maxine countered smoothly, "but I *am* interested in protecting my people."

Lucius adjusted the red handkerchief in his tuxedo pocket, as if the conversation was already boring him. The pocket square was the same bright, ruby red as the tropical flowers on the tables.

Lucius's dark, onyx eyes shifted down to look at Maxine. "Well, in that case, perhaps you should shut down your business. You're what? Coming up on sixty?" He snorted. "You know what, Max? I've even heard talk of you retiring."

Maxine ran a finger around the rim of her champagne flute. For anybody without military training, it would be an innocent action. For Maxine, it served to remind her how simple it would be to snap the stem from the crystal flute and bury the jagged point deep into Lucius's carotid artery. She could watch that smug look fade into pale realization—the moment he accepted that he'd never been superior to her. The energy expenditure on her part would be minimal, and Vladimir could have Maxine on a plane out of the country in less than an hour. She'd never face prosecution.

But when had Max left the Marines, she'd sworn an oath to herself that taking another human life was only ever to be a last resort. To think she had no other options at this point would be a fallacy. A lazy man pulls the trigger. A conscientious one finds another, better way.

"I *do* plan to retire," Maxine began, "but I have one final, parting obligation before I load up my wagon and head into the sunset. It's dealing with this pesky cockroach who calls himself The Phoenix. He needs to be squashed."

Lucius's dark eyes flashed. "Is that so?"

"He's scum," she nodded. "Protecting drug dealers, moving narcotics, trafficking women—and he even has a legitimate-appearing business as a front."

"He sounds like an opportunist." Lucius gave her a feral smile.

"He feeds off the misery of others," Maxine purred back. "He's the worst kind of criminal."

"Sounds like the type you'd get in bed with, Max."

Maxine shot him a glare. She knew it was only a matter of time before Lucius learned about Vladimir. She shot back: "He's twice the man you'll ever be."

Lucius leaned in closer to Maxine, and his voice dropped to a low snarl.

"Some advice for you: Shut down your rag-tag team, Rider—before I shut it down for you."

"It's you, *Lucy*, who have one week to shut down Titan Enterprises—or *we're* coming for *you*."

There. She'd now delivered her warning—and her entire team would hear the cue in their earpieces. From around her, Maxine's 'rag-tag' team materialized—Mica, Ryan, Reece, Vladimir, Mason, Claire, and Drake. Lucius took several surprised steps backward as they encircled him.

He'd suddenly learned that Maxine Rider was quite capable of infiltrating a high-profile gala with her entire, deadly team.

Lucius couldn't hide from her.

Maxine turned—leaving a red-faced, fuming Lucius Titan behind her.

AFTER MAXINE NODDED and walked away from the Rider team, everyone else dispersed.

Her back to Lucius, Maxine smiled as Vladimir approached

her. He looked formidable in his tuxedo—his bright, white hair perfectly coiffed on his head.

"Care to dance?" Vladimir asked.

"I need a drink."

Vladimir led her to the bar, where he ordered two neat vodkas and handed one to Maxine. They stayed at the bar, leaning on the counter side-by-side.

"You look beautiful," Vladimir murmured. "I like this side of you—with the hair and the dress." Then, the smile hardened. "Still, there's something very arousing about the pants and the gun on your hip, too. Very American Wild West." He lowered his voice as she leaned closer. "My favorite, of course, is no clothing at all."

Maxine sipped her vodka. Although she'd responded with only a slight curve of one side of her mouth, she'd appreciated Vladimir trying to lighten the mood.

"You got what you came for?" Vladimir asked.

"I did," she grumbled. "Lucius is a jackass."

"*Gorbatovo mogul ispravit.*"

Maxine grunted. "True." *A person can't change their character.* "We are who we are." The literal translation of the Russian proverb was far more poetic—*only the grave will cure the hunchback.* The English equivalent was about a leopard not changing his spots.

Maxine certainly thought Lucius more hunchback than leopard, although he did have claws.

"Thank you for coming," she said earnestly.

"We're a team."

Maxine downed her vodka. "I owe you that dance." She didn't care much for dancing, but she knew Vladimir liked to dance, and making the effort would express her gratitude and appreciation for him in a way she didn't know how to convey with words.

DRAKE FOLLOWED Claire into the hotel room, where he noted a single, queen-sized bed. Beige curtains covered the windows and a golden light shone from a lamp on the nightstand. On the chair sat an overnight bag.

"What are we doing here?" he asked.

Claire had directed him to this hotel after the gala, and he'd followed her past check-in and up to the room before asking her about it.

Claire slid her feet out of her shoes and began taking off her earrings. "I asked Mica to get me a hotel room under an alias. I can't go home until this thing with Titan is settled—but at least this way I can have a night off from that scrawny mattress and twin-sized bed at the office."

Drake thought that appealed as well, but he stood, unmoving, as he watched Claire. Her skin glowed softly in the light of the lamp, and her lips looked deliciously full and sensuous. Drake looked down at the floor, trying to coax himself out of the rising arousal he felt at being alone in a hotel room with this gorgeous young woman, who looked so desirable in her shapely cocktail dress. Looking down just directed him to Claire's rose-painted toenails, which caught his eye. He followed the line of her feet as it rose to her delicate ankles, and then her smooth calves. He watched the hem of Claire's dress brush against her skin and his breath hitched.

Drake needed to open the door—maybe pull out his phone and call Pete. Anything to distract him.

"Where's my room?" His voice sounded dry and foreign in his own ears.

"I was hoping you'd stay with me."

Drake gulped. "I'd like that."

He'd rushed to agree, although he didn't know quite what he was agreeing to do. Did she want him in the chair? Protecting her in her room? Did Claire want him to hold her in his arms all night? Or did she want something more?

He decided it didn't matter—he'd spend the night with her in whatever capacity Claire Maltisse wanted—and he wouldn't risk making a move, which might jeopardize his ability to spend even more time with her in the future.

Claire reached behind her back, unzipping her cocktail dress. She let it fall to the floor around her ankles. Suddenly, bare skin—covered only by black lingerie—filled Drake's view. The sight of it momentarily blurred his vision as his body shunted blood... *elsewhere.*

Her slender form was exquisite—with those lovely hips and the swell of her modest breasts. He was entranced.

As Drake's heart thudded with excitement, he was achingly aware of Claire watching him right back. Her wide eyes held a hesitant uncertainty. Did she think he didn't want her? He'd been aching to have her every moment he'd spent with Claire.

He realized he needed to kiss away her uncertainty.

"You're so beautiful." Drake drank in her appearance one last time before he stepped forward, enveloping Claire in his arms and pressing his lips against hers. Her soft, warm mouth invited him to deepen the kiss. As he did so, Drake ran his hands along the smooth skin of Claire's back.

Her hands explored him in return—working their way beneath his shirt. He felt their delicacy and their sinewy strength as Claire's fingertips moved along his ribs and back. When she finally released a soft, muffled groan into their kiss, Drake tugged off his jacket with haste. He stepped back to unbutton his shirt.

Claire bit her bottom lip as she watched him take off his shirt. Her hungry gaze fixated on him. Her cheeks were flushed, and her lips were swollen from their kiss. By the time Drake's shirt was off, she was pressed against him again—skin against skin... *almost.*

He reached around and released her bra.

As it fell to the floor, Drake pressed against her. Claire's head rolled back, exposing the soft skin of her slender throat. Drake kissed from her clavicle all the way up to her ear, relishing in the faint purring sound she responded with.

As they backed toward the bed, Drake removed the rest of his clothing. He slipped on a condom from his wallet as Claire lay down. Once more, he drank in the sight of her magnificence, before crawling onto the bed, hovering over her. Claire smiled, arousal lighting her expression...

...but there was something else. Hesitation?

Had she planned this night? Or just spontaneously invited him? Was Claire having doubts now? They'd never talked about intimacy.

Drake ached to resume their kisses and merge their bodies, but he didn't want any hesitation or regret from Claire.

"Are you sure?" he asked.

Her smile brightened. "Oh, *yes*."

He searched her eyes and found a mix of tenderness and heated desire within them.

Claire reached around him and pulled him down on top of her.

"Make love to me, Drake."

CLAIRE AWOKE STILL NESTLED in Drake's warm embrace. He felt so strong and secure that she thought she could lie in his arms for an eternity—except, of course, she had obligations.

If Lucius hadn't already had plans for the Rider team, he'd most certainly be making them now—after Maxine's confrontation with him last night. Rider SI had put forth a show of solidarity, and Lucius would want to eclipse Maxine's show of force with his own demonstration.

But, *no.*

Claire refused to lie beside the man of her dreams, after the most incredible night of her life, and crush her euphoria and libido by thinking of the inevitable danger lurking around the next corner.

She rolled over and adjusted her body, so her head rested on Drake's shoulder. She draped her long, bare leg over his. Drake's long fingers began moving up and down her thigh.

"Hey, gorgeous." His morning voice was deep and sensual.

When she kissed the skin of his chest, Drake gave a grunt of approval.

"I could stay here all night and day," Claire sighed.

"Stay as long as you like. You're running the show, sweetheart. There's no place I'd rather be."

A phone buzzed.

Drake reached over her, to the nightstand where their phones were charging.

"Yours or mine?" Claire asked.

"Mine—and it can wait."

He set his phone back down and settled back into their embrace.

As Drake ran a hand up and down her bare arm, he asked, "Anything you want to do while we stay here?" He stroked his fingers along the side of her breast.

Drake's heated gaze pinned Claire where she was, just as his touch sent a wash of desire over her. She arched her head back and stretched up to kiss him. Oh, his amazing kisses—so rich and full. Drake always responded to her tempo—soft and succulent, deep and passionate, or hard and needy.

Finally, she crawled on top of him, and he held both her hips with his hands. One hand moved up and tucked strands of dark hair behind her ear. His gaze roamed Claire's body—eyes, lips, breasts... and lower.

"You're so beautiful, Claire." His voice held a husky awe.

Warmth spread through Claire's cheeks before she slid lower on his taught, muscular body.

Drake sucked in a sharp breath.

"I have ideas on how to pass the time." She smiled.

MICA ANSWERED HER PHONE. "Well, well, well. If it isn't Cinderella, post-ball. How was your night?"

Beside Mica, Ryan sat in the passenger seat and glanced her way with an inquisitive eyebrow.

"I'll never tell," Claire replied on the phone.

"That good, huh?"

"Thanks for setting up the room," Claire said.

"Rooms. I set up *two* rooms," Mica reminded her.

"Yes? Well, we only used one."

"So I'd gathered. Where are you now? Walk of shame?" Mica teased.

"There is no shame to be found here. We're heading back to the office."

"Ryan fed, watered, and walked Bear this morning."

"Thanks. Where are you?"

Mica pulled into Maxine's driveway. "Meeting with Max and Vladimir. I'll check back with you later."

"Okay. Bye."

Mica turned off her engine. She and Ryan walked to Maxine's front door, where Vladimir greeted them—even before Mica knocked. He led them inside the house.

He was wearing jeans and a t-shirt. Mica was still adjusting to seeing the Russian mobster dressed so casually with Maxine, and she was still trying to reconcile this genuine and pleasant man with his fearsome reputation.

Ryan shook hands with Vladimir. Regardless of his past, Vladimir was on Maxine's side now, and that carried immense weight with everyone at Rider SI.

Mica and Ryan walked into the kitchen, where Maxine handed them each a cup of steaming coffee.

"Let's sit," Maxine said.

As they assembled at the table, she spoke, "So, the gala went as predicted. Lucius knows the gauntlet is thrown, and he picked it up instead of walking away. The Cronus Protocol is in effect, and Claire is done gathering information."

Vladimir sat with them, noticeably close to Maxine in a show of support. Mica would have called them a cute couple—if she weren't aware of how deadly they both were.

"So, we're ready?" Mica said.

Maxine pointed to a manila envelope on the table. "Yes—and part of being ready is a contingency plan."

The hair on Mica's neck stood on end. She knew what that implied. "No, Max."

"Hear me out," Max insisted. "Things are about to get more dangerous. By now, everyone knows I've been grooming you to take over the business. In an ideal world, that process should take six months to a year—or longer. However, we don't live in an ideal world, so you now have all of my protocols and client lists—both past and present."

Mica bit her lip. Maxine continued.

"This," Max placed one hand on the envelope, "is a will, should anything happen to me. You take over Rider SI, and David is part owner."

Mica squirmed uncomfortably in her seat. They'd had a solid plan for eliminating Lucius, but this business always mandated contingency plans. Yet, this sudden talk of Maxine's demise soured Mica's stomach. Max wasn't only a war hero and one of the most powerful women Mica had ever known—she was Mica's future mother-in-law. David would be devastated to lose his mother, especially after only recently repairing their broken relationship.

Ryan reached over and gave Mica a reassuring squeeze on her shoulder. Stoic and steadfast, he was Maxine's favorite and most trusted employee. His presence, and that platonic touch of approval, spoke deeper than words ever could.

Mica realized Maxine was waiting for a response. "I understand," Mica said. "I don't like it, but I understand."

"Good," Max nodded. "Now, let's talk about the next Rider meeting. I'm going to have everyone there, so we need to keep it organized and on target."

LUCIUS PACED HIS OFFICE, red fury clouding his vision.

The nerve of that woman!

"How did we *not* know she'd be at the gala?" Lucius demanded of Hoyle, who stood in one corner of the office with that maddeningly calm expression on his face and his arms clasped behind his back.

"It wasn't mentioned in any of the communications we were monitoring."

"I attended to show support to our clients—not to be blindsided by that bulldog."

"It shouldn't have happened, sir. We'll keep closer tabs on the Rider group."

"You'd better," Lucius growled. "I'm spending an exorbitant amount of money monitoring her and planning her death. It *needs* to end. Can you imagine if Rider interferes with Shiv Memon's party supplies somehow? We'd be out millions of dollars—not to mention the damage to my reputation. This thing with her *has* to end—*now*! I want it wrapped up before I meet with Abdul for the final transaction."

"We'll make it happen," Hoyle assured him.

A knock came at Lucius's door.

His masseuse poked her head inside the room. "You sent for me, sir?"

He'd almost forgotten he'd scheduled stress relief today. As the woman entered the room, Lucius dismissed Hoyle. The masseuse walked across the room toward the corner, where Lucius's massage table was folded against the wall. Her tight, red dress clung to her hips and rhinestone heels winked at him.

Lucius reached for his belt. "Skip the massage. Get on your knees."

rake pulled his jacket tighter around him as he stepped outside into the brisk, February breeze. His breath puffed in visible vapor into the cold night.

He was leaving Claire unguarded at the Rider office, but she had Bear and an entire arsenal at her disposal. Besides, no one knew about his impromptu meeting, so Lucius couldn't have planned a midnight attack.

A crescent moon curved a smile at him in the clear, night sky. In Greek mythology, Selene was goddess of the moon. She rode her silver moon chariot drawn by two, winged horses across the night sky. Under the circumstances, the glowing arc looked more like the devious smile of a Cheshire cat than a chariot pulled by mythical creatures.

Drake's footsteps echoed beneath him on the deserted Atlanta sidewalk. He stuffed his hands deeper into his pockets to keep them warm. Pete was relaxing in fifty-degree weather in Los Angeles right now, but somehow Drake enjoyed the crisp winter season.

In fact, he'd liked so much about Atlanta: The culture, the seasons, the Southern hospitality—and, naturally, his favorite part: Claire, with her slender curves and her mixture of strength and fragility, intelligence and insecurity.

Drake entered the Waffle House and spotted Catherine instantly. Despite her baseball cap and baggy, cotton clothes, Catherine's long, bleached blonde hair and prominent cheekbones were unmistakable—as were her wide, cherry-red lips.

Catherine hadn't ordered any food yet, and sat with nervous eyes darting around the diner. Drake shook his head. So much for being inconspicuous.

He slid into the booth and ordered cheese n' eggs with hash browns—scattered and covered.

When the waiter left, Drake demanded: "Are you okay?"

She looked up at him through long, coated eyelashes.

"It's been a year in this hell. What's another week or two?" Her tone was as bitter as lemon peel, and her English thick and broken. Catherine had told Drake when they'd first met that she was from Croatia.

"The Rider team is working around the clock to make sure that their plan to take down Lucius is airtight." Drake didn't know the details. He actually felt better *not* knowing them. If he remained mostly clueless, no one could torture any information out of him.

"Take down?" Catherine raised her head and looked at Drake.

"Arrested—with enough incriminating evidence to sentence him for five lifetimes."

"Arrested." Catherine scoffed. "He deserves death. Send him to God, who will send him to hell."

"This team doesn't operate that way," Drake cautioned. "They aren't going to assassinate anyone."

"Then they're the wrong team for the job." Her expression twisted in disgust.

Drake shifted in his seat. "Listen—when we agreed I'd help you, we'd planned your escape. This is better. When the Rider team puts Lucius in jail, you'll get your freedom, instead. Murder isn't a solution."

Catherine narrowed her eyes. "When will Rider attack?"

The waiter came and set down Drake's plate of food in front of him.

Drake waited for him to leave before speaking. "I don't know exactly." He wasn't lying, but even if he'd known the day of Maxine's planned retaliation, he wouldn't have shared that information with anyone—including Catherine.

Drake pushed his plate toward her.

"You should eat."

She'd been waif thin when he'd first met her, and she'd become even more gaunt with the stress of waiting for her escape.

Catherine shook her head. She stood, stepping out of the booth and looking down at Drake with contempt.

"When I'm free, I eat." She jabbed a finger into his shoulder. "Don't forget about me."

"Catherine," he pleaded, "stay and eat. Talk with me."

She placed a hand on his shoulder. "I don't want to be gone too long." Her voice softened, and her expression changed from frustration to pain. "Thank you for helping."

"I could take you to the Rider offices tonight. I could get you to safety."

However, even as he spoke the words, Drake knew Catherine wouldn't accept his offer. She wasn't alone.

She sighed. "That doesn't help my sister."

. . .

DRAKE WALKED QUICKLY BACK to the Rider offices. He felt miserable —the danger of the world around him seemed to be pressing in from every direction. It was as if he was riding a tiny boat through the Strait of Messina, with Charybdis to his right, seeking to devour him in a deadly whirlpool, and Scylla to his left, chomping those three rows of jagged teeth on each of her six heads.

Drake had promised to help Catherine—but the Rider's careful planning took time. Drake hated feeling so damn helpless, but a Rider-engineered plan to strike against Lucius Titan was infinitely better than anything he could have contrived on his own. The best, most logical action he could take now was to keep a protective bubble around Claire. She was the one who'd bring Lucius to his knees.

Still, Catherine had made her point—Drake wasn't doing enough, and he wasn't doing it fast enough.

When the elevator doors opened to the Rider offices, Claire greeted him. She was wearing gray pajamas, her hands on her hips.

"Midnight stroll?" She glared at him.

He pushed passed her, defeated. "Something like that."

Claire trailed after him. "Why the secrets, Drake?"

"It's not *my* secret," he sighed. "It's someone else's."

"What's her name?"

Drake stopped in the hallway, just outside the room where his office and makeshift bed were. "I can't tell you."

Claire's cheeks flared red, and the fire in her gaze burned hotly enough to scorch him. Claire apparently hadn't known it was a woman he'd snuck out to see—not until Drake confirmed it.

He ran a hand through his hair and rubbed the back of his neck.

"After everything we've been through, can't you trust that I'm not doing anything illegal? Or anything that would jeopardize what you're working on against Lucius?"

Claire put her hands on her hips. "After everything we've been through, can't *you* see that it's hard to trust this 'secret' isn't just another scheme?"

"That's not fair." His voice hardened. "I'm still here, Claire. I'm still backing you up every step of the way. That's proof of my solidarity."

"Maybe you stayed out of guilt." She tossed the words out carelessly, but he wasn't going to let them slide.

"Guilt is the reason I rescued you, Claire. It was my feelings for you that made me stay. Haven't I proven that to you?"

"We're in lock-down right now, and yet you're sneaking off to meet with another woman."

"You make it sound like I'm cheating. That's *not* what's happening here."

"Isn't it?"

Drake's temper flared. He tried to remind himself that Claire had many insecurities, and justification for all of them. She'd grown up in an insecure and unstable household, with no core family for support. When she'd tried to do the morally correct thing at MIT, she'd been kicked out for illegal computer activity. When she'd developed feelings for Drake, she'd found out he was working for the enemy.

Yet, he *had* proven himself to Claire, and so his patience was wearing thin. The constant vigilance of worrying about her safety was exhausting—always wondering when the next Titan strike would come.

He rubbed his throbbing temple. "I can't fight right now."

"Sure. We'll just postpone it until it's convenient for you."

"I'm exhausted. You're being unfair. We're tabling this." He stepped into his room.

Claire didn't sleep well that night. She woke tired.

Wasn't there some rule that a couple shouldn't go to bed angry? Were she and Drake a couple? They hadn't defined exactly what their relationship was yet, but the previous night's fight had made her feel ill to her very core. Claire didn't want to be a mistrusting, jealous partner.

Lying in bed, staring at the ceiling, she'd finally figured out that she didn't distrust Drake's motives. She just feared he might inadvertently compromise the mission.

Claire clambered out of bed and walked to the coffee machine in the employee break room, still dressed in her pajamas. She intended to make coffee. Claire liked one cup of coffee, first thing in the morning, and then she typically switched to tea for the rest of the day. More than one cup and she'd spend hours bouncing off the walls, instead of stationed before her computer screens with laser focus.

To her surprise, a fresh pot of coffee was already awaiting her. A sticky note sat on top of her mug.

I'm sorry.

Claire held the note as she filled up her cup with the fresh, steaming brew. The thick aroma whispered sweet nothings to her senses.

"Her name is Catherine."

Claire turned to see Drake leaning against the doorway, coffee cup in hand. He looked good in his suit pants and starched, white shirt—but the dark circles under his eyes suggested he hadn't slept well either after their fight.

"She was born and raised in Croatia," he continued. "Her parents scraped together enough money to send her and his sister to the States for a school semester. The host company claimed the women got room, board, and schooling—when, in fact, they took the girls' money and sold them to one of Lucius's handlers."

He sighed bitterly. "Apparently, that's how hundreds of women are trafficked—when their parents don't sell them outright. Catherine told me her awful story, and I made a promise I've yet to keep—to get her away from Titan Enterprises. Since I'm now on Lucius's target list, she's given up hope. I met with her last night to try to talk to her and tell her we're working on a solution." He rushed to add. "I didn't give *any* details, though."

Claire considered this story carefully, believing and trusting Drake.

Finally, she said, "If we can get her out, would she know anything about Lucius's organization that could help us take him down?"

Drake rubbed the back of his neck. "Undoubtedly—but she's too terrified to turn against him, and she has a sister he can use against her."

Claire nodded. Catherine and her sister would be better helped by the Rider team staying their course and taking out Lucius as planned.

"I'm sorry about last night," he added.

Claire set her coffee cup down and walked into his arms. "You're a good man, Drake. I shouldn't have distrusted you. I'm sorry, too."

He set his mug down and wrapped his arms around her. "Are we okay?"

"Of course we are. We're Perseus and Andromeda, right?"

He squeezed her close. "That's right."

⚓

MAXINE LOOKED around the room at her employees—those both physically present, and those on video conference. She didn't want the entire team clustered and vulnerable to an attack by Lucius, so she'd spread them out across different locations. Mica and Claire sat in the conference room with Maxine. Ryan, Reece, and Mason were at Reece's apartment. Barry and Billy were on screen—streaming from the location of their current assignment in London.

"Lucius Titan had the audacity to attack one of our own." Maxine knew how much the team valued Claire. Without her online reconnaissance work, they had no job. Without her off-site navigations, some of them wouldn't be alive today. "Lucius attacked our family."

"What's the plan, Max?" Reece twirled one side of his mustache.

"We need full retaliation—some of which probably isn't going to be legal. Vladimir Pronin has agreed to provide additional resources, since Lucius is the one who helped orchestrate an attempted assassination on him last year."

Ryan Walsh protested, "The Russian Mafia? We've been over this, Max. If we start aligning with criminals to fight criminals, we're no better than they are."

"You're gonna play boy scout after they took Claire?" Reece shook his head at Ryan. "Gloves are off, man."

Billy crossed her arms. "This has been going on too long, and I'm sick of sleeping with one eye open. We need to end this. End Lucius."

"Legally," Ryan insisted.

"I don't have enough on him for legal channels, Walsh. We can't hack his systems—Claire has tried. We eliminated AJ, but the info we got on him didn't incriminate Lucius. I'm empty-handed here."

Reece shot Ryan a frustrated look. "Whatever it takes, Max, I'm in. You got another Hellfire?"

Maxine grimaced. To get her hands on a Hellfire missile, she'd enlisted a retired CIA spook in South America. He'd fired it on an illegal drug manufacturing plant—and that action had escalated the rivalry with Titan Enterprises, and marked the beginning of Maxine's collaboration with Vladimir Pronin.

Max shifted her eyes toward Ryan. "What it'll take is me going to Russia. Vladimir and I have already chartered a plane. I'll see what resources we have and report back. I need all of you to continue the projects you're currently on in the meantime. Rider SI needs to stay afloat."

LUCIUS LISTENED INTENTLY to the Rider team conversation, recognizing the voices of most of Maxine's employees even though he couldn't see them.

Dissension had snaked its tentacles within her ranks. Reece and Ryan were in disagreement. Ryan Walsh had once been one of Lucius's men, but the boy scout—as even his partner Reece called him—had some sort of moral compass, which had prohibited him from continuing employment at Titan Enterprises. Now, in Walsh's employment with Rider SI, there were still lines he wouldn't cross.

Good. That only made them an easier target—and disagreements among them would make them even more careless.

Fear plagued Maxine. Lucius could sense it in her voice. He may not have crippled her to the extent he'd wanted by kidnapping Claire, but he'd rattled the bulldog. Now, Maxine was scrambling—rushing off to Russia to strengthen her alliance with the Russian warlord Vladimir Pronin.

Yes, that would come back to bite her in the ass. Vladimir Pronin didn't dish out favors. He'd *own* her.

Except Lucius planned to end the charade before Maxine had a chance to become an indentured servant to the Russian mob. Therefore, Maxine should actually be thanking Lucius. When he ended her, he'd end more than just her career. He'd end her miserable existence. That was cause for celebration. Lucius tipped back his Scotch and drank.

⁂

MICA WALKED beside Bill Sharp as they exited the building, with two of Sharp's bodyguards on either side of them. Aside from the fact that Bill made some of the world's most sophisticated weapons, he was also worth a billion dollars. He had admirers across the globe who wanted to emulate him, and enemies across the globe who wanted him kidnapped, or dead—or both, in indiscriminate order.

He was also the type of man who wore his fortune well. If people met Bill at a grocery store, they'd never know he was a billionaire. He'd even been spotted helping elderly women cross the road.

Mica wasn't his direct bodyguard. Her job was oversight. She reviewed travel routes and personnel assignments. She'd found Bill liked to bounce ideas off her that were often unrelated to his own protection. As such, she usually worked beside him throughout the day unless he was traveling overseas.

"How did your meeting go?" Mica had spent the day working in a vacant office while Bill Sharp met with a US general.

"Exceptionally well. They liked the drones."

Mica adjusted the briefcase in her hand. The drones he referred to were of the same type that Ryan and Reece had once protected, back when Lucius had attempted to steal one of them.

"Claire will be happy to hear that," Mica said. Claire had wanted her very own drone, but Maxine had explained curtly that she wasn't spending half a million dollars for a shiny new toy. Instead, Claire borrowed them occasionally from Bill.

"Does Claire like the nanoparticles?" Bill asked.

"She does. She's giddy as a toddler in a Chucky Cheese."

"I want a video."

"She knows."

Bill tapped his suit coat pocket. "Oh, I left my phone..."

Mica halted when Bill stopped walking. A bullet whizzed by them, striking a nearby car with a loud *thunk* as it sunk into metal.

"Sniper!" Mica lifted her briefcase to shield her head and Bill Sharp's body.

Pedestrians screamed.

One of Bill's bodyguards began herding Bill toward his Cadillac Escalade on the curb. He opened the rear door of the black, bullet-resistant Escalade and ushered Bill inside the vehicle.

The other bodyguard pulled his weapon, taking aim at Mica. Jolts of fear stabbed along her spine like a thousand tiny pinpricks. A traitor had been lurking in their midst all this time.

Yet, this wasn't the first time Mica had faced an armed attacker —and she had training and experience at her disposal.

Bill dove inside his vehicle, and the first bodyguard closed the door.

Mica didn't have time to draw her weapon against the traitor, so she hurled her briefcase at him instead, dodging left. The gunman missed Mica with his bullet, and it shattered the window of a nearby storefront. As he prepared to reset his aim, Mica ducked as she spun closer to him. She lashed out a leg into the man's knee. He grunted and, as he fell, positioned himself for Mica to bring her knee up into his jaw.

She felt the crunch of his teeth jarring against each other. As he fell back, she kicked the gun out of his hand.

Mica dashed back to Bill's Escalade, where the first bodyguard was opening the driver's side door. She dove into the driver seat of the Escalade and yanked the door shut. She didn't need keys, since Bill always carried the spare and the car would detect the proximity of the key fob.

As she pushed the button to start the engine, the first body-guard climbed in the passenger seat.

Outside the vehicle, the traitorous bodyguard struggled to his feet. The street was now empty, as pedestrians had taken cover inside buildings or were cowering behind street vendor carts. Mica pulled away from the curb and rapidly accelerated. The faster she left the scene, the faster everyone's safety would be ensured.

In the back, Bill tugged on his seatbelt, but remained low in his seat.

"Jeez! I've never been the target of an assassination attempt on my life." His face was pale. "I'm shaking. I always knew it was possible, but..."

Mica glanced in the rearview mirror as she gripped the wheel. Her heart pounded against her ribs. "We'll get you to safety."

She didn't say it, but Mica knew the hit had actually been directed at her, not Bill. As expected, Lucius Titan had made his next move. Knight to Rook four.

16

———

*D*rake drove Claire in his black Explorer down Peachtree —or *one* of the Peachtrees. This town had so many roads named Peachtree, Drake couldn't keep them all straight. Georgia was, after all, The Peach State.

As Claire sat in the passenger seat, she toyed with a remote control. They'd finished the errand she'd wanted to run—picking up supplies from the hardware store.

"Another drone?" Drake asked.

"A decoy."

"What for?"

"Just a precaution."

Drake eyed her focus on the remote while her computer sat in her lap. He glimpsed the screen, which showed an interactive map and what looked like a street view camera. It wasn't of Peachtree—at least not the Peachtree they were currently driving on.

Drake wondered if Claire's brief responses were the result of intense concentration, or if she was intentionally leaving him in the dark. Other than the gala, this was their first outing since the kidnapping. They'd spent their days in the office together, mostly working—her on Project Titan, as he called it, and the Cronus Protocol, whatever that was. Drake, meanwhile, had continued studying private security from a variety of sources—Maxine's company manuals, discussions with Ryan Walsh over lunch, and searches on the Internet.

When Drake wasn't educating himself and expanding his horizons, he recorded his voice-overs and kept up with his Hollywood contacts. He didn't know what life held in store for him once Lucius was behind bars, but he couldn't let his acting career dwindle into non-existence while he spent his time on the opposite coast. In Hollywood, out of sight was out of mind—and he risked losing the next good job the longer he stayed away from Los Angeles.

What was next?

He glanced at Claire again. They hadn't talked about their night together in the hotel. She'd been amazing—and the morning after, he'd held her in his arms until they'd needed to get dressed and check out of the hotel.

Claire had been so blissfully calm—as though a night of passion had soothed her restless soul. He hadn't wanted to disrupt her tranquility by asking about the long-term ramifications of what they'd done—or by begging for another night just like it.

Besides, he needed to wrap his head around his feelings for Claire before he could have a coherent discussion about that.

In the rearview mirror, a silver Tahoe suddenly caught Drake's attention as it accelerated towards them. Had the car been following them? Damn—a tail was probably something he should have detected, since he was Claire's security detail.

"I think we've got company—the bad kind."

Claire spun around to look. She gave a dismal groan, but her expression wasn't surprised. Had she been expecting an attack? If so, she hadn't shared that minor detail with him.

"Back to the office?" Drake asked.

"No."

The Tahoe accelerated to within inches of Drake's Explorer, and he barely sped out of reach before it touched the rear bumper. One good nudge to the corner of his fender would send the car into a tailspin. While the Explorer was robust, Drake knew the specs of his off-the-forecourt Ford didn't compare to those of Lucius's presumably decked-out Tahoe. Sure, the car he drove had tinted windows—but they certainly weren't bullet resistant like he imagined those of Lucius's fleet to be. Likewise, the doors weren't reinforced to withstand automatic weapons fire—or any weapons fire, to be honest.

"Brake hard and turn left here," Claire ordered, her nose back to her computer screen.

Drake swerved around another vehicle, braked hard, and then cut across the oncoming traffic. Horns blared angrily at him as he made the turn and straightened out. The Explorer was now heading south on Fulton Industrial Boulevard.

Their pursuers made the same turn, but cars on the intersection slowed them down. Drake managed to gain some distance between them as he drove. On either side of the Explorer, offices, manufacturing plants, and distribution centers blurred as they sped down the boulevard.

"Hard left on Boat Rock Road." Claire's voice sounded strained.

Drake suspected this was as her first car chase as much as it was his. He tried to take steadying breaths and urged himself to view this like one of his stunt double scenes. The only difference was that every safety precaution was taken on set, and nobody was *actually* trying to injure or kill anyone.

Drake passed an eighteen-wheeler, slowed, and swung hard left. The road narrowed and a roundabout came into view.

"Right at the roundabout."

"Why do I get the impression this car chase isn't a surprise to you?"

"We both knew he was going to come after us eventually."

"But you knew about this." When he shot Claire a frown, she countered with a sheepish grin.

"Not exactly *this*, but I had a hunch."

Drake swung the Explorer into the parking lot of an apartment complex. He looked around frantically. "Sweetheart, we're sitting ducks here." His voice was an irritated growl.

"Trust me," Claire reassured him. "I've gotten the Rider team through many a car chase—you can ask any of them." She never lifted her eyes from her screen, or her hands from the controller.

"You need to enlighten me on the plan, Claire." He'd have to live through this before he could phone any of Claire's colleagues to substantiate her claim.

Lucius watched the car chase from a camera mounted on the front dash of Hoyle's Tahoe. Hoyle had his phone on the vehicle's Bluetooth, so Lucius could communicate with him while he watched.

Hoyle took the same left Drake and Claire's Explorer had taken. The road was deserted.

"Where'd they go?" Lucius snapped, leaning forward in his desk chair as he inspected the mounted screen in his office.

"Must've turned off the road," Hoyle replied. "They'd have slowed down for that. We'll catch 'em."

The Tahoe proceeded cautiously through a roundabout, which offered a good view of the road ahead. No cars.

"We'll check the parking lot of that apartment complex," said Hoyle.

"Dawson, what's your ETA?" Lucius demanded. He had another driver en route to box Drake and Claire in.

"Five minutes out. We're Southbound on Camp Creek Parkway," came the reply.

"There! There!" Hoyle shouted.

As Lucius watched the Tahoe turn and straighten, Drake's Explorer came into view. Hoyle gunned the engine, closing the distance between them. Drake took a hard right, back onto Fulton Industrial Boulevard headed north. Dawson's vehicle came at them from Camp Creek Parkway, making a U-turn to follow Drake back north. A gas station zipped in and out of view before Lucius found himself looking at Drake's bumper again.

As Hoyle's Tahoe pulled alongside Drake's car, Lucius could only see the road and shoulder of Camp Creek Parkway through the camera.

"We've got him boxed in," Hoyle said.

The road was two lanes, but the shoulders made it wide enough to fit three vehicles parallel to each other. Drake's car came in and out of view as the two Tahoes sandwiched the rear end of the Explorer.

"Take the shot!" Hoyle barked.

A gunshot rang through the phone. As Hoyle's car slowed, the Explorer became wholly visible, jerking wildly and turning sideways before plummeting headfirst through the railing and over the bridge.

Hoyle's car came to a stop.

"They're over the edge—sinking into the Chattahoochee."

Maybe they'd survive. Maybe they wouldn't. Lucius wished he

had a view of the river. He'd have liked an instant replay of the SUV sailing through the air.

"Okay. Clear off the bridge before the authorities arrive. Change vehicles and see if you can monitor when they're fished out downstream."

"Copy that."

MAXINE AND VLADIMIR drove to the private airstrip.

"Are we really doing this? Are *you* really doing this? There's no going back."

"*Da*. We're a team, Max. *Komanda*." He emphasized 'team' in Russian.

Max adjusted her grip on the wheel. "Do you ever think about retirement? Think about leaving this all behind?"

"I took over the mob to maintain an empire, and to use it to protect my family. I've done as much as I can do. Now, it's time they protect themselves. Natasha will make a good replacement."

Maxine knew Vladimir's past well. Despite his many dark deeds, he'd ultimately used his sinister acquisition of power within the Russian Mafia to build a shield around his family. He'd acknowledged that his organization spread drugs and crime, but he'd also emphasized the 'organized' component of organized crime. He'd molded that component like supple clay—turning the Russian Mafia into something more cohesive and less violent than it had been under the rule of his predecessors. In his rationale, controlling an evil beast within a cage—offering it occasional sacrifices—was better than unleashing it.

Maxine couldn't condone the things Vladimir had done in the interests of survival, but she could at least bear witness to the fact that he hadn't degenerated into an immoral, cruel man—despite the horrible conditions life had tried to drown him in.

"Likewise, your successor seems capable," Vladimir said.

"Mica McMillan? She's young and needs experience—but with time, she could certainly take the lead."

"What if this leadership role paints a bullseye on her back, like it did yours? What about David?"

Maxine thought of her son—a brilliant emergency room physician engaged to Mica. "I think he understands my work—Mica's work. He's been supportive of her every step of the way. He'd support her in a leadership role." Maxine felt like her relationship with David was mending. As part of their reconciliation, he'd also been meeting members of her team and getting to know the men and women of Rider SI. He'd seen them in action and understood the valuable work they did. He'd also seen Mica's passion for the organization—not to mention that a man in love always supports his woman's endeavors.

Vladimir reached over and took Maxine's hand in his. "Everything will work out as it should."

She parked the Crossover at the private hanger. She hoped he was right. She really hoped that everything would work out—but that didn't supplant her worry that it could all go to hell.

LUCIUS WATCHED the camera feed of the airplane parked on the tarmac. He sipped his Scotch and reclined in his office chair. This strike would be part three of his four-pronged attack on Rider SI. The attack on Claire and Drake had reached completion when they'd careened over the bridge and into the Chattahoochee River.

Mica McMillan still had to be dealt with, since she'd frustratingly survived the sniper attack carried out earlier today. AJ had similarly failed to eliminate her several months earlier, which had resulted in her joining Maxine's organization and using the Rider SI resources to have the FBI arrest AJ. She was slippery—but not much of a danger without Maxine's support. For that reason,

Lucius would decide later how much more effort he'd invest into killing her.

The attack on Ryan Walsh and Reece Owen would take place in a few hours. Ryan Walsh needed to be eliminated—he'd worked for Titan Enterprises briefly and had used that connection to help send AJ to prison. That was a bitter harvest Walsh was long overdue in reaping.

On screen, Lucius stared at the Eclipse 550. It would be a shame to destroy a three-million dollar, dual-engine jet—but it hadn't been paid for with Lucius's money. The airplane belonged to Vladimir Pronin—and had probably been used for many a drug smuggling escapade. Since Vladimir's drug trade interfered with Lucius's own business, killing Vladimir at the same time as he killed Maxine would put a nice dent into the Russian Mafia's pocketbook.

Perhaps one of the many infuriating traits Maxine possessed was her self-righteous sense she was somehow *better* than Lucius. She thought she was more moral than he was, because she didn't protect drug smugglers, didn't help crime syndicates transport illegal women of leisure, and didn't bribe, cheat, or steal.

Yet, there she was—walking right onto the plane of the head of the Russian Mafia.

Lucius leaned in and observed Maxine's slight limp through the camera feed. Yes, it was definitely her then, and not a decoy. Maxine had cast all her foolish morality aside to get into bed with the Russian mob—literally *and* figuratively. Well, she was about to learn that even the mighty Pronin couldn't protect her.

Lucius chuckled out loud at the irony. Maxine Rider—patron saint of pompous principles—was abandoning her pious ways only to die in the plane of a drug-smuggling crime lord.

Hah! Ain't life grand?

The airplane ramp closed with Maxine and Vladimir on board.

The plane on the screen in front of him suddenly burst into a bright explosion. Red flame preceded black, billowing smoke.

"*Yes!*" Lucius exclaimed. "Take *that*, you sanctimonious bitch!"

Two birds, one Hellfire.

He'd used the same weapon she'd used against him—to destroy that drug production facility in Argentina. The irony felt poetic. Maxine wasn't the only person with resources.

Lucius rewound the footage to watch it again... and again... He smiled wider each and every time. Maxine and Vladimir had climbed onboard, and—*boom!*

Sweet, sweet victory.

RYAN SAT at a table at Northside Tavern and texted his wife, letting her know he'd be home late. He was still working.

A live band played the blues in the pub, but Ryan and Reece sat at the opposite end of the establishment, away from the music. Blue dome lights hung above the bar. It smelled blissfully of Guinness and greasy fries.

The response came swiftly, *K, love you. Stay safe.*

Reece sat across from him, staring down into an empty glass. "This sucks. We should've just attacked Lucius the day he went after Claire." His words were slow and slurred. "Seek and destroy."

"We're not Tomahawks."

Reece sniffed, wriggling his mustache. "It'd be simpler if we were."

"We have to be smarter." Ryan ran his fingers along the condensation on his own glass.

Reece snorted. "A lot of good all this preparation will do if we let Lucius pick us off one-by-one." He ran his hands through his hair. "I hate the waiting."

"It's all part of the game."

"It shouldn't be a game. These are people's lives."

"I don't disagree—but if we don't treat it like a tactical game, we'll get careless. If we let fear, or frustration, or impatience win, we'll make mistakes. We can't afford mistakes—not for us, or for our loved ones."

Reece shot him a narrow-eyed glare. Reece was on-again, off-again dating a woman, and Ryan knew Reece's emotions ran deep for his girlfriend—even if Reece didn't admit it himself. Despite the fluctuations in their relationship, Reece didn't date any other women when he was anguishing in bachelorhood, during the periods between fallouts with Jess. That behavior was unprecedented in all of Ryan's years of knowing Reece.

"Your constant logic is a pain in the ass."

Ryan chuckled, but quickly sobered his mood.

"What do you think of Drake?" Reece asked.

Ryan leaned back and crossed his arms. "I was mad at him at first—but he didn't kidnap Claire, and he's not the reason she *was* kidnapped. He made a poor career choice by joining Titan, but I'm the last person who can fault him for that."

"What do you think about him being with Claire?"

"I try *not* to think about it," Ryan grumbled. "She's like a little sister to me—but she does seem to like him, and he seems to have a calm temperament, which balances her boisterous spirit. I'd like to see her happy with somebody."

"Well, if we all die bringing down Lucius, nobody gets to live happily-ever-after."

"Then let's make sure that doesn't happen. You ready?" Ryan started to stand.

"It's that time?"

"It is."

When they walked out of the bar, the crisp, night air struck Ryan's cheeks. Reece leaned on Ryan for support.

By the dim light, twelve men stood in the parking lot. Based on their leather jackets and nearby means of transportation, they were a biker gang. Apparently, Lucius had outsourced this attack. This made sense—since he wouldn't want Ryan and Reece's death traced back to Titan Enterprises.

The bikers' hard gazes fell on Ryan and Reece.

"Reckon it's our turn?" Reece asked.

"Seems it is."

Reece straightened. "Rangers lead the way."

17

___

*M*axine was dead.

Lucius practically bubbled with giddy delight. He thought he might burst into song—transforming into a Munchkin and dancing to *Ding Dong The Witch Is Dead*. Had he ever experienced such satisfaction?

Lucius had orchestrated multiple strikes in a short time span, and they'd all been successful. A Hellfire missile had incinerated Maxine and Vladimir. Claire and Drake had plummeted over a bridge—and Lucius had been told by his men that they'd seen an ambulance on-scene along the banks of the Chattahoochee River. Ryan and Reece had reportedly taken a beating and gone to an emergency room.

The only irksome hit had been the one on Mica McMillan.

She hadn't been eliminated by the sniper he'd arranged for her. At least the attack had been staged in Bill Sharp's presence. That weapon's manufacturer would hopefully now think twice about continuing to support any company with Mica in its employment.

In fact, with Maxine dead, Bill Sharp might be looking for a new partnership for his security detail. Maybe Lucius would be getting a call from him.

Lucius scrolled through his playlist. Perhaps *Another One Bites the Dust* would be more appropriate. His former employer—a retired Israeli Special Forces operative turned security contractor—used to love to play that Queen song after a successful mission.

Lucius's assistant's voice came through his office intercom. "Mr. Patel is here to see you, Mr. Titan."

He depressed a button on the desk phone. "Excellent. Show him in."

As the door opened, Lucius stood and adjusted his tie. He strode around his desk to greet Abdul Patel, who looked as polished and collected as ever. "It's wonderful to see you again." His eyes landed on the briefcase. The down payment.

"The pleasure is mine," Abdul purred. "Few people can accommodate Shiv Memon's desires. I'm happy to have found your organization. The shipment assembly is coming together, I trust?"

"Yes, yes—we'll have your order, and the private delivery location you requested will be in place by your deadline."

"Splendid."

———

Drake watched tears stream down Claire's face as he held the black umbrella over her. The priest's voice was drowned out by the sound of falling rain. As Rider SI had predicted, Lucius had lashed out against them. In a twelve-hour timespan, he'd launched offensive attacks on Mica, Maxine, Ryan, Reece, Drake, and Claire.

Claire wore a black dress. A black dress and black hair. She wasn't the same, bubbly woman Drake had unsuccessfully wooed many months ago. She'd matured under the weight of everything she'd faced—but her pain and suffering seemed to magnify the feelings Drake had for her. He wanted to shield Claire from the ugly, callous world—a world where a young woman had been manipulated by an ignorant man, then kidnapped and almost tortured.

Yet, Claire had never been naive. Drake knew about her past and the poverty she'd overcome. She'd known the ugly, callous world since a young age—more than he ever had.

Now, Claire Maltisse stood at a funeral for the woman who'd been a friend, role model, and parental figure for so many years.

Across from them and the casket stood Mica and her fiancé David—Maxine's son. David held an umbrella over them with a white-knuckled grip and an angry scowl on his face. Not sad or pained—just pissed. Standing beside David, Mica had her arm looped around his elbow, staring down at the dark, cherry red casket.

Ryan Walsh seemed to be unable to look at Maxine's casket. Rather than join the attendees, he leaned against a cane by a distant tree, letting the rain soak his black suit as he sulked there, all alone. His arm was snug in a sling, and half his face looked bruised and swollen. Reece, Drake had been told, was in no shape to even attend the funeral.

Drake felt like a schmuck. The feud between Lucius and Maxine predated his employment at Titan Enterprises, but Drake still felt like his role had served as some sort of catalyst to what had happened.

Claire had been kidnapped—and then unstoppable events

had cascaded into a sniper attack, car chase, plane explosion, and a funeral.

When the priest finished with a psalm, Drake escorted Claire to his Explorer. He opened the door for her. After she climbed in, he opened the driver's side door, collapsed the umbrella, and sat out of the rain. With the doors closed, he heard only the beating rain on the windshield.

Claire pulled tissues from her purse and wiped under her eyes. "Oh, my gosh. This stuff is amazing! I bawled my eyes out the entire time."

"Acting trick." Drake winked at her as he started the car, turning up the heat. A thin, wax stick of menthol under the eyes had guaranteed Claire's tears.

"Do you really think Lucius would send spies to Maxine's funeral?" Drake asked.

"Most certainly. He's probably reveling in his victory. Yes—he'd probably demand photos of everyone in mourning."

Lucius wouldn't get everyone, though. Maxine had wanted a fake funeral, but she hadn't wanted too many Rider employees in one place. As such, Ryan sulked in the perimeter, Reece pretended to be too injured to attend the funeral, while Billy and Barry remained on assignment. The show must go on.

"Do you think Lucius will buy it?"

"Yes—the team did great," Claire said.

Mediocre acting, thought Drake. "David looked angry, not upset."

"I think it worked though. He's been estranged from his mom for a while. He's bound to be pissed that someone tried to kill her."

"I'm sorry, Claire."

She stopped stripping off the menthol and stared at him.

Drake continued, "I'm sorry for everything I've put you through. Everything that led up to the funeral." He looked out of the window.

Claire placed a hand on his cheek. "The truth is that I mostly forgave you as soon as you rescued me. All of this crap with Lucius isn't your fault. He may have even kidnapped me sooner if it hadn't been for you—which would have interfered with us taking AJ down. Not to mention, if you hadn't cultivated your fake relationship with Titan's company, nobody would have rescued me." She sniffed. "Well, Max would've found me eventually, but who knows what condition I'd have been in—or what information Lucius would have got out of me."

She sighed. "I shouldn't have gotten jealous about Catherine. That's my own demon to expel." Her watery eyes met his. "So, Drake—you are forgiven. Also, I'm sorry."

He smiled at her. They'd already reconciled that issue, but she apparently still held remorse. "I like that you care about me."

"More than I've ever cared about anyone."

Drake leaned toward Claire, judging the tender moment needed to be sealed with a kiss. Kissing Claire felt like coming home. When their lips met, all the problems surrounding them dissolved and life was bliss.

The Explorer rocked as Ryan suddenly opened the door behind Drake and climbed into the back of the car, interrupting their kiss. He tossed the cane aside and pulled off the sling. "Whew—it's warm in here. I like it."

Drake suppressed an irritated sigh as he leaned back from Claire. Judging by Ryan's dimpled smile and amused expression, big-brother Walsh knew exactly what he'd interrupted.

Ryan leaned forward and inspected his face in the rear-view mirror. "This movie make-up is so realistic—and it didn't even wash off in the rain."

Drake thought the disguise appeared passible from a distance —in the rain. Drake was no make-up artist, but Ryan's face did look like he'd taken a beating.

Claire had explained that Ryan and Reece could have taken

down a dozen of Lucius's hired bikers in hand-to-hand combat, but they'd had to *look* like they'd lost—or at least tied the fight. As such, they'd taken a few punches, pretending to be more injured than they actually were. They'd finished the fight with everybody on the ground—bikers and Rider SI employees alike—but alive.

Lucius had hired bikers, and they weren't the kind to report failure, just in case they'd have to return their fee. They'd likely told Lucius that they'd beaten Ryan and Reece to a pulp. Ryan's visible injuries at the funeral would support that claim, and Lucius would count it as a victory.

The destruction of Vladimir's jet was another victory in Lucius's eyes—but, in reality, the video feed had been cleverly manipulated. Lucius had never seen Maxine and Vladimir climb *off* the plane moments after boarding it; before the explosion.

Yet even compared to that, the best deception had been Claire's decoy car. She'd had an Explorer identical to Drake's rental car outfitted with a remote control, which she'd used while Drake was driving to escape Lucius's men in those two Tahoes. When Drake and Claire had pulled into the parking lot of that apartment complex, Claire had the decoy vehicle pull out. It was the decoy car that had gone over the bridge—and thanks to the tinted windows, Lucius's men had never seen that nobody was riding inside the Explorer.

While the decoy was costly—as all these deceptions had been—they'd allowed Lucius to believe he'd won.

Mason, meanwhile, had been instrumental in everything that had unfolded.

He'd been the one to tamper with the video feed of Vladimir's plane exploding. He'd been the one to install the remote control in an Explorer looking exactly like Drake's rental car. In addition, unbeknownst to Lucius, he'd been lurking in the parking lot of that pub to join Ryan and Reece in fighting the dozen hired bikers.

Lastly, Mica's escape hadn't been as "lucky" as they'd made it seem. Lucius had contracted out the sniper hit—presumably to reduce the chances of responsibility falling back on him—but it's not easy to hire a Lithuanian sniper without the Russian Mafia hearing of it. Vladimir had replaced the Lithuanian hire with his own employee, Sonya—who'd been given instructions to attempt the hit at the same time the Lithuanian had been expected to. To minimize risk to surrounding bystanders, she'd only taken a single shot.

It almost hadn't been enough. The traitor on Bill Sharp's security team was an unexpected surprise. Mica had demonstrated the value she provided to Bill Sharp as his security advisor by promptly dealing with him.

So, unbeknownst to Lucius Titan, the Rider team had actually won this battle—but the victor of the final engagement, and the overall war itself, still had yet to be decided.

CLAIRE PULLED OUT HER PHONE—HER backup phone, which wasn't traceable by Lucius's organization.

"Who are you calling?"

"Maxine's burner phone. I'm telling her I sent flowers, and I expect the company to reimburse me for them."

Drake chuckled as he pulled away from the curb.

"How was the funeral?" Maxine asked when she answered Claire's call.

"Wet," Claire replied. "How are you?"

"Happy not to be six feet under. I'm glad Mort came through for us."

Mort was Maxine's acquaintance—a former-CIA agent. She'd used him to launch a Hellfire at the Argentinian drug factory a while back. Ironically, when Lucius hit the black market to find someone able to kill Maxine Rider—without it being traced back to Lucius, of course—Mort had been the one to take the job. He'd promptly called Maxine to let her know there was a hit out on her—and with the advanced notice, Maxine had been able to stage everything; right down to the video feed Lucius received being tainted with few seconds of loop, so Lucius had never seen Maxine and Vladimir leave the plane moments before the Hellfire missile hit.

In the end, everyone was happy. Maxine and Vladimir lived, Mort got to use explosives *and* get paid for doing so, and Lucius was none the wiser to their scheme.

"It was surreal being at your funeral," Claire admitted.

"Do you know if Lucius saw it?"

"Not directly—but I suspect he had spies." Claire turned in her seat. "Ryan, did you see anyone you recognized from Titan Enterprises?"

"No."

"He says 'no'," Claire said to Maxine.

"How are you holding up?" Maxine asked.

"I've learned that when I'm cooped up and isolated because I'm *hiding* from someone, I enjoy it much less than when I'm cooped up and isolated voluntarily—just being my typical, antisocial self."

"I can understand that. Is Fitzy behaving himself?"

Claire glanced at Drake as he drove. "Yes. He's helpful—and charming."

Drake grinned.

"How long are you going to make him your indentured servant?" Claire asked as a follow-up, absently tapping her fingers on the armrest.

"I don't know," Maxine said warmly. "How long do you want me to keep him around?"

Claire let out a nervous chuckle—but she wasn't sure how to reply with Drake listening in. "I don't know."

"Has he asked about going home?"

"No."

"Has he talked about missing California?"

"No."

"Then why don't we worry about sending him home when he's ready to go home?"

"Okay."

"In the meantime, we've got a counterstrike to finish implementing."

"Yes, ma'am."

⁂

CLAIRE SAT in the Rider SI conference room with Drake and Ryan.

On screen were Maxine, with Vladimir, and Reece, with Mason. Claire had felt huge relief the moment she'd seen Maxine. Even though the funeral had been staged, it still highlighted the very real threat Lucius had posed to Maxine's life—to all their lives.

"We're secure?" Maxine asked.

Like she has to ask?

"No listeners." Claire had removed the spyware Lucius had clandestinely installed to spy on their conference calls. When she'd first discovered it—during her routine check of computer security—Maxine had made the strategic decision to leave it in place—so they could throw Lucius off.

Claire pulled up the three-dimensional schematics she'd created of Lucius Titan's main operations building. The image projected onto a screen large enough for all those on the video call to see clearly.

"These schematics are brought to you by hours of my personal research, as well as vital information from both Drake and Ryan."

Claire sucked in a breath and spoke in a serious baritone:

"Many sacrificed to bring you this information." She cleared her throat and looked expectantly around the room—receiving only blank stares in response. "No? No takers for the Star Wars reference? 'Many Bothans died'? No one gets the Death Star reference?" She sighed, shaking her head as the attempt to lighten the mood fizzled and died.

Drake winked at her.

Claire then went through the three-dimensional building diagram layer by layer—starting with the helipad on the roof, then Lucius's offices and executive offices on the fifth floor, the conference rooms and overnight accommodations on the fourth floor, more offices on the third floor, followed by equipment rooms and servers on the second floor. The first floor was mostly open space—meant to look impressive, with a fountain, marble floors, and the twenty-feet-tall statue of a phoenix. The basement of the building was comprised largely of garage space, with the subbasement housing the air-conditioning and heating units.

"Security?" Maxine asked.

"Entry and exit are badge access only through the front door, rear door, and basement-level parking. The ammunitions room is on the first floor. Cameras are posted at all entrances and elevators, as well as hallways and even many offices—including AJ's."

It seemed there was no one who could escape Lucius's watchful eyes.

"Minor obstacles for *you*," Ryan said to Claire with a twinkle in his eye.

"The badges, yes," she responded, before admitting, "Unfortunately, I can't remotely hack the cameras—and these aren't *just* cameras. They feed back to a server with facial recognition software."

Reece unleashed a low whistle.

"Now," Claire continued, " Lucius doesn't have access to any federal databases for facial recognition, but he can program them to alert security if they detect any face he's had preprogrammed into the system."

"I bet Ryan's on that list," Reece said.

Claire nodded. "I bet he is, too."

Since Ryan had worked for Lucius, he posed a security risk. Ryan had, in fact, given Claire quite a bit of insight into what she'd just presented to the group.

"In fact, as thorough as Lucius is, I'd be surprised if he didn't have all of us labeled as intruders in his system."

"We'll operate under the assumption he does," Maxine said.

"So, where's our entry? Where's the weak spot?" Reece demanded.

"Cleaning crew," Vladimir and Ryan said in unison.

Everyone stared at the Russian mob boss.

Vladimir shrugged. "It's always the cleaning crew."

Claire clicked to the next slide. "So, the cleaning crew comes on Monday, Wednesday, and Friday." A van with *Peachtree Cleaners: 'We get you peachy clean!'* painted on the side appeared on screen. "They enter through the subbasement level, park, and clean from eight until midnight."

"How many of them?" Maxine asked.

"Two cleaners."

"Vladimir and I will go."

The room erupted in protest, with both those in the room and the others on the conference line objecting to Maxine infiltrating Lucius's building.

Claire kept quiet—since she already knew about Maxine's plans.

Vladimir just chuckled.

Claire glanced at Drake, noting the worried expression on his face. Was he concerned about Maxine as well? Nobody wanted her risking her life on this escapade—and Maxine *would* be risking her life. Lucius was ruthless, and he'd already demonstrated his willingness to kill Maxine and anyone else who got in his way.

"This is how it is," Maxine said firmly. "Get behind it."

Everyone fell silent.

"Claire, continue."

18

*M*axine and Vladimir entered Lucius Titan's building via the rear entrance, as planned. They were wearing the standard, faded, peach-colored coveralls of the Wednesday night cleaning crew, and swiped into the building using the badges Claire had forged for them. They worked—and the door swung open the moment the sensor chirped. Vladimir carried a silver box as he entered the building, and Maxine followed with a metal toolbox.

They walked to the cleaning supply closet beyond the elevator, silently passing numerous mounted cameras on the way. After they'd grabbed cleaning carts, the two of them wheeled them out of the closet and down the hallway. Maxine set her toolbox on top her cart, while Vladimir set his box inside his.

With calm strides, they pushed their carts to the elevator. Maxine pressed the 'up' button and Vladimir pressed the 'down' button. They'd rehearsed their respective roles in the infiltration of Lucius's building several times—and Claire's schematics had been precise, right down to the location of the cleaning supply closet.

Maxine took the elevator to the third floor, before heading down the hallway to AJ Schlau's former office. The former Titan employee had been incarcerated for several months now—and Maxine knew she was taking a gamble that the office even still belonged to AJ.

He'd been arrested, but there were many appeals to go through before he faced an actual conviction—and AJ might even be permitted to post bail. If Drake's inside intel had been correct, Titan Enterprises had been keeping AJ's office intact for that very reason—not knowing if he'd be able to wriggle out of the charges levelled against him and return to his previous role.

That was a gamble, though. Lucius wouldn't want anything illegal being traced back to him—and even if AJ dodged charges or conviction, the stench of his accusation might be more than Lucius was willing to put up with.

If that office did now belong to some other employee, Maxine would be forced to improvise.

She reached the office. Maxine opened the toolbox and pulled a plastic case the size of a compressed powder make-up case. She opened it and pressed her thumb into the gel, then pressed her thumb against the fingerprint analyzer on the door of AJ's office. It took a moment, but then a green indicator light flashed.

Next, Maxine pulled out a black cylinder the size of a small flashlight and uncapped the top. She held it up to the retinal scanner.

The Rider team had managed to get AJ's fingerprints and retinal scan during a pseudo medical exam, after Mica had defeated him in hand-to-hand combat several months earlier. Now, that technology was getting the acid test.

There was a clunk. The door unlocked.

Success number one.

Maxine pushed the door open—and then hesitated, listening for the sound of alarms. Not that she expected Lucius to have loud, archaic alarms installed. If she'd tripped some kind of alarm, she probably wouldn't know about it—not until Titan's goons surrounded her and she was staring down the barrel of a Beretta.

She spoke into her live earpiece, "Claire, I'm in."

"Great," the earpiece spoke back in Claire's excited tone. "USB in the port, okay?"

Maxine sat in front of AJ's computer. She wriggled the mouse to get the computer out of stand-by. A prompt for a password came up. Maxine typed in the password Claire had given her. When it worked, Maxine released a breath she hadn't even realized she'd been holding.

Good thing AJ's home computer and work computer had the same password.

"It worked," Maxine reported.

"You say that like you had doubts," Claire replied into Maxine's earpiece.

Maxine ignored her—instead plugging in Claire's USB drive, which had been pre-programmed with an application to access the files and servers AJ had been granted access to.

This was the difficult part. Claire had needed somebody to place this drive in AJ's computer on site, because she couldn't bypass Lucius's firewall remotely.

It seemed to work, though. The application began downloading AJ's files—all of them.

.   .   .

Lucius stared at the security monitor in speechless disbelief. Maxine Rider was alive!

He should have known a Hellfire missile, into a stationary plane, was too easy a target. He'd correct that mistake soon enough.

But first—why would she be dumb enough to enter his building?

Lucius had state-of-the-art facial recognition software built into the cameras of the Titan Enterprises building, and it had been pre-programmed to alert him if any of the Rider team intruded. As soon as Maxine had entered the building, one of Lucius's security team had alerted Hoyle, who was now stood in Lucius's office.

Hoyle bent over Lucius's desk and pulled up security footage on his boss's laptop to show him. Lucius frowned as he watched it.

Maxine must have thought she was *so* clever coming in dressed as the janitor—accompanied by Vladimir Pronin, no less. The Russian must be short on personnel for him to make this appearance himself.

Ah, but Vladimir *had* no personnel anymore—because just like Lucius believed Maxine was dead, the Russian Mafia thought their leader had also been killed. Lucius had even heard that Vladimir's niece, Natasha, had already taken over the business.

This meant Vladimir no longer had the weight of the *rossiyskaya mafiya* behind him.

A smile crept across his face. While disappointed they'd survived the Hellfire missile, this allowed Lucius a rare opportunity—it wasn't often you got to kill your nemesis twice.

Even better, Lucius had Maxine and Vladimir trapped like mice—and they didn't even know it yet. He watched on screen as Maxine stole AJ's files from his computer, while Vladimir lurked in the basement. Doing what? Setting bombs?

Lucius couldn't be sure what Vladimir was doing, because he

kept popping in and out of blind spots in the camera system. He couldn't access anything valuable down there, though. The servers were housed on the second floor, not the basement.

So, it didn't matter. His men would stop Vladimir before any damage was done—but Lucius wouldn't make the mistake of underestimating the pair of them again.

As soon as he'd been informed that Maxine and Vladimir had breached his building, Lucius had called in every off-duty employee to his facility. His men would have every exit secured before they made the move to apprehend Maxine and Vladimir—and, just in case they'd brought explosive devices, Lucius had also ordered his helicopter to land on the roof. It was in flight at this very second—and in the next ten minutes would be landing on the roof, poised to fly him to safety.

Lucius continued to watch Maxine as she busied herself in AJ's office, calmly stealing his information—and completely ignorant to the fact that Lucius was bringing in reinforcements even as she sat there. She looked ridiculous in her coveralls and baseball cap, with her untamed hair sticking out of the sides and back. Did she even brush that crow's nest? She was speaking with someone through an earpiece—probably that blue-haired minion of hers, Claire. His video feed didn't include audio, so he couldn't hear what she was saying—but as he watched, Maxine pulled out one USB drive and inserted another.

"Oh, no you don't."

Lucius tapped on his keyboard, using his computer to remotely disconnect AJ's computer from the company's internal servers. He wasn't about to allow Maxine to plant some kind of virus or Trojan horse on Titan Enterprise's computer network.

As for the other USB drive—the one Maxine was shoving into her cargo pants, beneath her coveralls—it didn't matter. She wouldn't leave the building with it—not alive.

A knock suddenly sounded at Lucius's door.

He looked up, momentarily startled. The masseuse entered. She looked back and forth, from Lucius to Hoyle. "Your appointment, Mr. Titan?"

Had he made an appointment for tonight?

It was entirely possible he'd done so—and simply lost track of it in the confusion of all the simultaneous operations he was running. He looked up at the young woman—standing in her tight yoga outfit, with her long, blonde hair and large, voluptuous lips. He wasn't going to take time out for a massage or other extracurricular activities—not right now—but he would take her with him. She'd be costly to replace if Maxine and Vladimir actually managed to blow up his building.

Lucius turned to Hoyle. "Get a team to the basement and stop whatever that Russian buffoon is doing down there. I'm heading to the rooftop."

***

"Claire, how are we doing?"

Claire pressed a button on the console to unmute her comms piece and replied to Maxine. "Peachy. You've only got fifty of Lucius's men storming the building like they think they're saving the President."

"How much time do I have?"

"Three minutes."

Claire heard shuffling, followed by a door opening. She envisioned Maxine leaving AJ's office and making her way back to the elevator.

Drake shifted in his seat beside Claire. She glanced at him, hunched in the tiny space they shared in this surveillance van, half a mile away from Lucius's building.

How bizarre was her life? What woman would break up with

her boyfriend and *then* be forced into spending every day of the following week with him?

More puzzling, she hadn't been able to squelch her feelings for Drake—not when he was so constantly charming and attentive.

After she'd spent the night with him in that hotel—lost in the glorious throws of passion and pleasure—she'd ended up being thwarted by her own insecurity. She wanted so much more from Drake—but was painfully aware that the hourglass of their time together had almost run out.

His obligations to Maxine and his friend Catherine would soon be met. Would he stay then? Would he want to? Would he consider it if Claire actually *asked* him to? But *could* she ask a man to leave his home and his career? For *her*?

Maxine had given Drake explicit instructions to serve as Claire's bodyguard. Claire had performed surveillance on innumerable occasions and Maxine had never insisted on her having protection before. Claire understood the explanation Maxine had given—that she wasn't taking any chances that Lucius might outwit them on this mission.

When Maxine had given Drake the assignment to protect Claire that morning in the cabin, he'd replied with: "Not a problem." Just like that.

As if Maxine had asked him to uncork a bottle of wine, or fix her another cup of coffee. *Not a problem*—as if he wasn't risking his life by being a part of this operation.

What did that mean?

"Is she going to make it?" Drake asked.

Claire put her microphone on mute. "She'll make it. The plan is solid."

Drake stared at Claire's screen, which showed the camera view of the front and rear of the building. "That's a *lot* of armed goons gathering."

"It is, isn't it?" Claire's eyebrows lifted. "I vet everybody who submits an employment application to Rider SI—and I've only found one worthy hire in the last six months. *One!* You wonder how Lucius recruits so many men."

"I imagine his criteria is less stringent."

Claire wondered if Drake was also referring to the fact that Lucius had hired him. Maxine *did* have strict criteria: A good military record—the length being less important than the standard of service—or some other relevant law enforcement experience, plus a college degree, a background check without evidence of morally corrupt actions, and trusted references.

"Could be the healthcare plan," Claire suggested.

Drake gave her a wry grin. "Titan Enterprises does offer an excellent benefits package."

"I'm in the basement," Maxine interrupted.

Claire pressed the button to un-mute her.

"Copy that." She hated being blind. Her video feed consisted of only the cameras she'd placed external to the building. She couldn't see what was happening inside.

Claire turned to look at Drake. "I guess you'll have to give up those benefits, since your boss is going to jail."

Drake leaned in closer. "He's not my boss anymore. I'm currently unemployed—but if Maxine is hiring...?"

Claire snorted. "She won't hire *you*—you're an actor."

"Yeah, and a damn good one," Drake retorted, "and judging by this video feed, she *needs* a good actor. Did you see those two walking toward the building with scowls and determination? I'm not surprised they were spotted. They might be dressed like cleaning crew, but they don't *look* like janitorial staff. Not the coveralls or mops, but their expressions and body language. They *looked* like they're on a mission."

"Oh? You could've done better?"

"Hell, yeah! You've got to *think* like an overnight janitor. Put earbuds in. Do a little swagger. Bob your head as you walk down the hallway. Slouch the posture a bit. You've gotta *work the role*."

Claire grinned. "*You* work the role?"

"I *rock* the role. I could teach the entire Rider team."

"Claire, you're *not* on mute," Maxine snapped.

"Oh, shit." She reached for the button.

"Drake, you're hired," Maxine said.

Claire froze and stared at the screen. There was no further movement, since all of Lucius's men were already inside the building. Slowly, Claire turned toward Drake and gaped at him in surprised disbelief.

Drake looked as surprised as she did.

"Are you seriously thinking about working for Maxine?" She paused. "Well, I guess it would be Mica, now."

Maxine was planning to retire—and Mica would be the next CEO.

"I am," Drake nodded. "Does that bother you?"

"What about your acting career?"

"I love acting—but if I'm acting for a private security company, one who helps people, then that's more intrinsic reward than acting for fame and fortune." He leaned closer to Claire. "But listen—I won't do it, not if you don't want me to."

Claire swallowed. She'd spent these last few days of proximity with Drake waffling between two extremes—contemplating either pushing him away, or begging him to stay. Yet, he'd needed no pushing or prodding in either direction. He'd made his decision, and he'd persisted in it. Drake had made a mistake, owned it, and made amends. He'd won over the rest of the team—people far warier and more cynical than Claire was.

Plus, Drake was charming, fun, honorable—and tough.

"I *do* want you here," she said.

Drake cupped her chin and leaned in for a kiss. Claire met him halfway.

The back of a surveillance van was probably the least romantic place she could think of kissing a man—but somehow, it seemed to fit them perfectly.

And why not? They were unconventional—quirky and improbable. Despite the location, or maybe because of it, their kiss felt sublime—smooth, deep, and sensual.

When they separated their lips, Drake smiled—widely and engagingly.

"I love you."

"Claire!" Maxine snapped. "Your mic is *still* live. For God's sake, get your head in the game!"

Claire pressed the mute button. "I love you, too."

Lucius sat in his airborne helicopter while his men surrounded Maxine's van in the basement parking garage. The camera view he watched came from headgear on Hoyle—his lead man on the ground. Lucius's men had automatic weapons raised and pointed at the van. All the other exits were covered. Maxine and Vladimir had no other means of escape. Hoyle called out for the intruders to exit the vehicle slowly.

Lucius stared at the screen intently, waiting for Maxine to emerge from the back of the van where she was hiding. He wanted to see the crushing look of defeat on her face before he forced her to surrender. Before he killed her.

The seconds ticked by—but Lucius saw no movement on the screen.

Fine. If she wanted to go down in a blaze of glory, he could accommodate that.

"Open fire!" Lucius hollered over the thumping of the helicopter blades.

The dozen Tavor X95 automatic rifles trained on the van erupted. The blasts lit his screen with flashes of light and smoke.

His men didn't cease fire until all their magazines were empty. Bullet casings littered the floor. The van was riddled with holes.

Survive that, Maxine Rider.

Hoyle eased his way to the back of the van, weapon poised to fire. Two other men stepped into view, wrenching open the rear door.

Empty!

Outrage and fury surge through Lucius. On screen, he suddenly saw how Maxine and Vladimir had parked their van right over the sewage drainage system. The van's floor had a large hole in it, pre-cut, which they'd obviously crawled through to escape.

Lucius pounded his fist on the wall of the helicopter. Beside him, his frightened massage therapist recoiled into the corner. When he'd pulled himself together, he searched the sewer schematics on his laptop. Only one route existed which Maxine and Vladimir could take. They might have a good head start on Lucius—but he had a helicopter.

"Head southbound," Lucius ordered the pilot.

Lucius set his laptop on the seat beside him and pressed his face to the helicopter window. He looked out at the dark land-scape below. A floodlight from the helicopter danced over the tree-tops and buildings.

As they passed over an SUV, parked at the exit of the sewer system, Lucius cried: "There!"

Suddenly, the SUV turned on its lights. It pulled onto the road, wheels spinning, and Lucius's pilot banked the helicopter right to follow it.

Mouse? Meet cat.

"Hoyle—I'm tracking them. Westbound on Highway 78. I want all men en route."

"Yes, sir."

Maxine wouldn't get away—not this time.

. . .

MICA ENSURED everyone was in position—Ryan and Reece in sniper position, Eddie half a block away, and Claire and Drake in the surveillance van on the opposite side of the warehouse. Dorian was within walking distance of the rendezvous point.

From her position on top of a tractor-trailer, Mica saw Maxine and Vladimir pull into the parking lot of the warehouse, near the large, metal, halide area lights. The deep thumping of helicopter rotors filled the air.

Lucius.

Headlights from other vehicles pierced the night horizon. Beside Mica, Mason shifted his binoculars. "There's a whole army of assholes on Max's six."

They knew Lucius would be enraged enough to deploy all the forces he didn't otherwise have on assignment, but it still jolted Mica to see the Devil's cavalry in full force.

Cold sweat trickled down Mica's neck, following the line of her spine in a chilling, serpentine pattern.

The Rider team was massively out-gunned—even if they counted the few FBI Eddie had brought with him. If the next fifteen minutes didn't go according to plan, tonight would end in a blood bath.

19

From the air, Lucius watched Maxine park her van in a dead end near a private warehouse.

Only it was *his* private warehouse, he suddenly realized.

The hair on his neck prickled. This warehouse was where he'd planned to meet Abdul Patel in a half an hour to make their exchange. Did Maxine know about his business dealings with Abdul? Is that why she'd chosen to come here? What was she scheming?

Still, Lucius had her outnumbered ten to one. Even if she brought the entire Rider team, Maxine had no chance of winning.

Lucius had Maxine trapped.

"Box her in," he ordered Hoyle and his men on the ground,

speaking through his headset over the thrum of the helicopter blades. "Nobody fires unless fired upon."

There'd be no watching this on video, since Lucius wanted to ensure he witnessed Maxine's execution with his own eyes. No room for error this time. She stood on *his* turf. *His* storage facility —in an industrial park with no residences or businesses nearby.

The pilot landed the helicopter away from the power lines, but near the warehouse. Lucius clambered out, even though the helicopter blades hadn't stopped whirling yet. Cool spring air whipped around him, and he shielded his eyes from airborne particles of dirt and leaves as they flew into his face.

Lucius strode past the black SUVs parked in a semicircle around Maxine's van, all registered to Titan Enterprises. His men had weapons leveled at Maxine and Vladimir, who'd had exited their vehicle. Lights shining from above the parking lot cast a yellow glow over the pair of them. They both appeared to have shed their janitorial outfits. Maxine wore cargo pants and a maroon T-shirt, while the Russian mobster was dressed in blue jeans and a grey, button-down shirt. Maxine's expression appeared calm and unafraid. Lucius snorted. It was just like the arrogant bitch to *not* recognize when she'd been beaten.

"Evening, Lucy," Maxine greeted him.

"It's over, Max." Lucius opened his arms wide, basking in his glory. Seven cars and fifty men surrounded them. Even if Maxine had some of her rag-tag team nearby, they were no match for his sheer force of numbers. If Ryan, or Reece, or Mason attacked, Lucius and his men could end Maxine and Vladimir in seconds.

"Give me the USB drive."

Maxine pulled it out of her shirt pocket and raised it in the air. Hoyle stepped over and retrieved, snatching it out of her hands. He stepped back and handed the drive to Lucius. He dropped it into his own pocket.

Then, Lucius pointed one finger, shaky with rage, at Maxine.

"You *lost*."

It infuriated him that she was so inferior, and yet had eluded his first assassination attempt. No matter—Maxine Rider would die tonight.

"Actually, I believe this is checkmate," Maxine said coolly.

Lucius glanced around. Tractor-trailer cargo was parked near his warehouse, which stood dark and silent in front of them. Otherwise, there was no other presence to suggest Maxine's words were anything other than a bluff. She was delusional.

He gave a sardonic snort. "You have nothing, Rider. No files. No proof."

"I have that crate filled with women you're trafficking," Maxine responded. "I've half of these men standing here, who'd turn against you in a heartbeat when they realize you're no longer a threat to them or their loved ones."

Nervous glances swung in his direction. Lucius's men shifted their weight on their feet. A cold sweat suddenly trickled down Lucius's neck.

But Maxine was *wrong*.

Each one of his men had their own demons to hide. None of them were innocent, and none of them could risk turning on Lucius and being exposed themselves. Some of them even had families. They wouldn't risk Lucius's wrath against their loved ones.

So, *no*.

Maxine had nothing. Nothing so powerful that it could turn his own men against him. Her words were just a ploy—probably an attempt to get him talking and inadvertently confess to something. Claire was likely recording their conversation somehow.

Lucius was on the verge of giving the order to kill her when someone called his name. He looked over in shock—only to see Abdul Patel walking toward him with a briefcase.

The exchange.

One million, in cash—in one-hundred-dollar bills. *Lucius's* cash.

Abdul looked around at the armed gunmen with an inquisitive expression. "Do I—*ahem*—need to be concerned about the integrity of our business deal?"

"Of course not," Lucius tried to regain his composure. "I'm dealing with these maggots. Your women and drugs are in the warehouse."

Lucius took the outstretched bag. It contained twenty-two pounds of cash. He had Hoyle hand Abdul the key to the freight containers, where the women and drugs were being held.

Lucius then turned to Hoyle—about to order him to kill Maxine and Vladimir...

...when suddenly, the men around him began to convulse.

Every. Single. One of them.

Like something out of a horror movie, all his gunmen and operatives began to flop and twist, their bodies falling to the ground, writhing uncontrollably.

* * *

CLAIRE WATCHED through the camera mounted on the dash of Maxine's van. On the screen, she watched as Lucius's men went rigid and fell—thousands of volts of electricity stunning them into unconsciousness. She cringed, knowing from experience what the crackling electricity of a stun gun felt like.

Maxine exhaled audibly into her microphone. "About time, Claire. I was worried you were going to let them shoot us before you activated the nanoparticles!"

"Magnificent," Vladimir cooed as he surveyed the unconscious bodies.

Drake sat in stunned silence, before saying: "That was so cool! I knew they weren't solar power-generating nanoparticles."

"Sorry, Max," Claire apologized, still staring at her screen. "The activation to initiation took a lot longer than in the practice models I'd run."

"How'd you *do* that? And how is Lucius still standing?" Drake demanded.

Claire put Maxine and the group back on mute while she explained. "While Maxine was less-than-inconspicuously sneaking around AJ's office—all in front of the security cameras—Vladimir was in the basement accessing the air-conditioning and heating ducts. He pumped nanoparticles throughout the building. The particles then coated everything—including all of Lucius's men who'd ducked into the office to collect their weapons before chasing down Maxine.

Her eyes flashed. "Lucius is only unaffected because he fled the building to get into his helicopter. Maxine and Vladimir are unaffected because they changed out of their nanoparticle-infested coveralls, so they wouldn't get stunned with electricity."

Outside the warehouse, Maxine and Lucius confronted each other.

"What have you *done*?" Lucius demanded through clenched teeth.

"My invisible stun gun," Maxine replied.

"Impossible."

But the twitching bodies of his men were a compelling argument against that.

"Maxine got the idea from her son, David," Claire explained to Drake. "After they'd reunited and bonded over their plot to take down AJ, David bought the entire team Tasers. As a physician, he said he wanted to encourage less-than-lethal means of offense. At the time, we'd all thought it was cute, if impractical; but it gave me an idea. I pitched it, and Bill Sharp then made the development possible. The weapon is made up of a cloud of millions of nanoparticles—smaller than a particle of dust—which coat anything they come into proximity with. These ones were engineered to transmit an electric frequency when broadcast correctly —like a cloud-based Taser."

Claire's brow furrowed. "Although, hopefully none of these men had pre-existing heart conditions, which would predispose them to complications when getting shocked."

But then, the concern left her face. "Bill Sharp is going to *love* this. I filmed the entire thing, so he can have the footage for his marketing materials. In exchange for use of his nanoparticles, he wanted evidence of their utility. Now, he has proof they work in the field, to show his next defense contractor during negotiations."

A voice rang across their speakers.

"FBI! Hands in the air!"

On the screen, Claire and Drake watched Eddie Finch and a dozen agents in uniform converge on the scene. Accompanying them were Mica, Mason, and Reece.

Lucius stood there, dumbfounded. Reluctantly, he raised his hands in the air.

The Indian, Abdul Patel, grabbed his briefcase of cash and took off at a sprint.

"Freeze!" Eddie boomed as he took aim.

Abdul never slowed.

Eddie fired a single shot.

Abdul fell, face forward, onto the pavement.

Drake's eyes widened as he watched the action unfold on screen.

"Who *was* that?"

"Ah," Claire nodded. "That was Dorian. He works for Maxine."

"What? He just got shot!"

"Yes—and no. The gun was fake. Blanks. We needed Lucius to think Dorian died so Dorian's alias—the black-market Indian broker—wouldn't get blown."

"Alias?"

"Dorian has been meeting with Lucius to set up a meet—money in exchange for women and drugs."

"The briefcase?"

"Yes. Dorian brought the cash. It's on loan from Vladimir for this sting."

Drake nodded as the pieces fell into place. "So, he and Lucius made the exchange—and you got it all on camera."

"Yep."

Drake leaned in closer to the monitor. "Dorian has some wicked acting skills."

"Yes, he does."

"So, what did Maxine steal from Lucius's office, then? What's on the USB? I thought that was the evidence we needed."

On screen, the FBI began cuffing the moaning men on the ground.

Claire answered Drake's question. "There's probably nothing on there. I mean, Max downloaded a few files, but Lucius isn't dumb enough to keep anything incriminating on his office servers —and if he did, the FBI now has the USB to back up their case."

"So, the infiltration of Lucius's building was all a ruse," Drake realized. "To centralize the Titan Enterprises team and contaminate them all with the nanoparticles?"

"Bingo."

Drake chuckled. "You've got the coolest job."

Another gunshot rang out.

Drake and Claire jumped to their feet and gaped at the monitor screen. They watched as Lucius Titan fell to his knees, before crumpling face-first to the ground. Behind Lucius stood a blonde woman—holding a smoking gun.

"That's Catherine," Drake gasped.

The FBI agents aimed their weapons at her and hollered for the woman to drop the weapon. She did so, even as her face remained flat and expressionless.

Claire scrambled to get on the phone and call 911—summoning an ambulance to the warehouse location. Drake continued to watch the screen with horror.

When an FBI agent wrestled Catherine to the ground, she didn't protest. Only calm acceptance crossed her face. She was free.

Drake slumped down heavily into his chair.

RYAN DROVE the Explorer away from the warehouse. Beside him, Vladimir sat quietly.

"Does it feel good to be free?" Ryan asked.

"*Da*. Better to be a free bird than a king in captivity."

"Is that a Russian proverb?"

"Norwegian. I'm looking forward to anonymity."

"The world thinks you're dead ever since that plane explosion. You've got a new identity now."

Vladimir's new identity was part of the reason Ryan was driving Vladimir away from the warehouse. He needed to *not* be swept up in the FBI's investigation—because, if he was, the reports would then inadvertently reveal to the world that Vladimir's violent demise had been faked.

That's why Ryan had been tasked with sneaking Vladimir off scene. With dozens of Lucius's men still writhing on the ground, and the FBI focused on detaining the armed assailants, it hadn't been difficult for Ryan and Vladimir to sneak away.

"It was very generous of you to help Maxine and me," Vladimir spoke softly as they drove. "It was very generous of Jenna to convince her parents to sell their resort to me."

Jenna's parents owned a resort in Antigua, where Maxine and Vladimir were planning to escape to. Her parents were in their seventies and looking to sell it—and they preferred the idea of selling to a couple of entrepreneurs, rather than developers who'd want to demolish the resort in favor of building another gaudy, ten-story hotel.

Maxine and Vladimir were the perfect couple to take over the business. They'd keep the resort as it was, and Vladimir had moved sufficient funds to a number of offshore accounts before his 'demise' so they'd be able to hire more help running the place, and invest in the upkeep of the resort.

"As long as the visitation parameters remain, we're good," Ryan said.

Jenna had wanted to ensure she could still visit the island resort with Ryan and her son Cal.

"*Da, da,*" Vladimir snorted. "The Rider team is always welcome. Maxine would be heartbroken if you didn't visit—and I've been perfecting my Italian cuisine, so I need guests to serve it to, *da*?"

"I like Italian food. Once your living in Antigua, you'll have to add Caribbean cuisine to your arsenal. Jenna makes a good ducana. It's steamed sweet potato and coconut, wrapped in banana peels."

"*Khorosho,*" he agreed with a smile. "Caribbean food is next."

Ryan pulled into Maxine's driveway. "You need anything else?"

"No, no. You have been most generous."

Ryan extended a hand, which Vladimir clasped with both of his.

The Russian shook it firmly. "I'll take good care of Max."

Ryan gave a slight, reassuring smile. "I know."

MAXINE WATCHED Mica and Mason approach, while Lucius was driven away in an ambulance. She wondered if he'd be taken to the emergency room where David worked. She pulled out her phone and sent a quick text to David that events were over. Titan's men were in custody, Lucius had been shot and was en route to a hospital, and the entire Rider team were safe.

Eddie paced the scene, talking to his supervisor as his men continued their arrests. Maxine saw him watch the ambulance drive away, lights and sirens blaring.

"Well, shit—I didn't see that coming."

She walked toward Dorian, towering over him as he lay on the ground. "You're clear to rise from the dead."

Dorian smiled as he rolled over. Clambering to his feet, he brushed off his suit. "The sacrifices I make for you, Max. I'll have you know; this is a Brioni Vanquish." His voice reverted to its usual, silken British accent. Then, his tone sobered, "I've seen the young woman who shot Lucius before. She's one of his trafficked women."

Maxine stretched her lips in a thin, grim line. "That's what Claire told me." She turned and gestured toward Mica. "Dorian—meet Mica McMillan."

He extended a hand. "Delighted. Max tells me you're her successor."

Mica shook it. "I hope I can be half the boss she is."

"You'll do splendidly from what I hear."

Next, Dorian turned toward Mason and extended his hand again. "Mason! Always good to know you've got our backs."

When they'd finished shaking hands, Maxine leaned closer.

"Dorian—listen. I'm sorry for making you reactivate an old alias and be a part of all this." Initiating the Cronus Protocol had required tearing Dorian away from his family and putting his life in danger for the duration of the sting against Lucius. He'd originally accepted employment with Maxine with the caveat that he wanted to be on protection detail—without any undercover operations. Yet, she'd needed to use his background and skills for this mission. As Abdul, Dorian had created a trail of evidence the FBI could use to finally hold Lucius Titan accountable for his atrocities.

"It's fine, Max. It was all for a good cause. No harm done. I needed to kill that bloody alias once and for all, anyway."

"Dia's okay?"

"Dia is enjoying college freedom—and probably many other freedoms a father doesn't dare think about. I'm sure I've caused my family some worry, but they'll be better as soon as I give them word this assignment is over."

Mica shook her head in awe. "Your role in this was magnificent. What's your background?"

"Ah, my dear." Dorian smiled with a twinkle in his eye. "That is currently above your clearance level. Check back with me when *you* run Rider SI."

20

"I can't even believe the relief I feel, now that everything is over." Claire sat across from Drake at the Atlanta Seafood Company. "Look at us," she laughed. "Having dinner like a normal couple!"

They sat at a red, tabletop booth opposite each other—a delicious spread of sushi stretched between them. The atmosphere was perfect. One nearby wall in the restaurant had a mural of men working on the docks. On another wall hung a shining, blue and white swordfish.

Since that dramatic night, they'd learned that Lucius was recovering from his gunshot injury—which had been directly to his spine. He'd live—but would be a paraplegic for the remainder of his life. Lucius had no sensation from his bellybutton down to his toes.

When he'd recovered sufficiently, he'd be spending the rest of his days in jail—although the question was how long those days would be. The Rider SI team had already begun taking bets on how quickly one of Lucius's own clients would arrange a hit on him, to prevent him from turning over evidence which might incriminate them.

Catherine had divulged everything she'd known to the police in exchange for a lighter sentence for her attempted murder. Catherine's sister had been freed from Lucius's captivity, along with a dozens other trafficked women. Many of Lucius's own men had also begun turning over evidence to save their own skin from the FBI investigation.

Maxine was working toward retirement, and Vladimir had let news of the missile strike on his private plane spread internationally—until, as far as the authorities and the Russian Mafia knew, Vladimir Pronin was officially listed as deceased.

Only his niece and the Rider team knew he'd secretly retired to Antigua.

Drake had decided that helping other people gave him more fulfillment than acting, and that he could use his skills to help the Rider team. He'd given up the lease of his apartment in Los Angeles and had moved to Atlanta permanently—where Claire and Bear had welcomed him with open arms... and paws.

"The dinner is nice," Drake agreed slyly, "the ambience is pleasant—but it's the company that makes it delightful." His eyes flashed. "It's also nice to be sleeping in a house instead of an office building."

"To your new place of employment." Claire raised her glass. "May it always be separate from your house—but feel like home, and us part of your family."

With a smile, Drake touched his glass to hers. "Cheers."

THREE MONTHS LATER

MAXINE SAT ON THE BEACH, watching the rhythmic, mesmerizing roll of the small waves on the sand. She sat beneath an umbrella, but still felt the sun radiating off the surface of the tropical beach. She smiled.

The knowledge that her nemesis was disgraced and behind bars gave her a deep sense of security. The tranquility of this island shore, along with Vladimir resting beside her, also filled her with a feeling of calm she hadn't experienced since—ever.

"You're happy, *da*?" Vladimir reached over and took her hand.

"I can't believe it, but, *yes*. I'm happy. I'm relaxed." She turned to look at him through her sunglasses. "*We* did this."

"'Man has it all in his hands, and it all slips through his fingers from sheer cowardice.' That's from *Crime and Punishment*. But you —who are not a coward—grabbed hold and clasped your dreams." Vladimir shook his fists into the air.

"Are you saying I have it all?"

"A tropical island retirement? No longer being estranged from your son?" He chuckled. "A charming *vozlyublennyy* who makes you laugh?"

"Oh? Where is this *sweetheart* you speak of?"

Vladimir rose out of his chair and leaned over her, his large torso blocking Maxine's view of the beach. His lips spread in a slow, feral smile. "Do I need to remind you?"

She slid her sunglasses off her face with a smile. "Every. Single. Day. *Moy vozlyublennyy*."

He pressed against her, before sealing her lips with a heated kiss.

. . .

SIX MONTHS LATER

Maxine sat across from Lucius Titan at the Hays State Prison. He sat in what looked like a worn, second-hand wheelchair, his spine erect and his face expressionless. When the correction's officer had wheeled him into the visitation room, Maxine had seen Lucius's full orange jumpsuit and the emaciated shape of the loose, bottom half of his body. She'd read in the paper that the bullet had nearly severed his spine.

Catherine had, no doubt, intended to kill Lucius when she'd fired the handgun at him—one she'd snatched from one of his own men as he'd lain twitching on the ground. Instead, she'd condemned him. Lucius Titan would never again tower over a woman, and never force himself on one again, either. He was now destined to the rest of his life stripped of power and dignity—rotting in prison.

"Hello, Lucy."

He folded his fingers together over the table, looking pleased.

Pleased because she'd come to visit him? Pleased because he thought she was there for information?

Or pleased because he was scheming revenge?

"Maxine Rider. It's been, what? Six months?"

"I knew you were preoccupied with the trial and physical therapy, so I didn't want to bother you," Maxine responded coolly.

The truth was that she'd actually been busy enjoying retirement with Vladimir. Only when she'd finally had to return to Atlanta did she take the time to come to the Hays State Prison.

"I'm short on company." Lucius raised his hands and gestured to the empty visitation room. "I'm sure a man of my talents, with the business you run, could be of service to you. I know all the players."

Maxine scratched her chin with a grin. "I'm not sure I can afford your consultation fee."

"I'm sure we can come to an agreement."

Maxine grunted.

Lucius tilted his head to one side. "Do I look like I can do a damn thing with money? I've got three life sentences ahead of me—with no chance at parole."

"So, you want to deal in favors?"

"Is that so bad?"

"Depends on the favor."

Maxine was retired—but if Lucius didn't know that yet, she wouldn't bother to inform him. But Mica...

Mica might need Lucius's distasteful type of expertise moving forward, and Mica would be cautious enough not to be swindled.

Lucius smiled—and it was surprisingly calm and non-malevolent.

Maxine looked at her watch. "Do you realize we've been in the same room for five minutes and you haven't threatened me?"

"You bested me, Max. I suppose I could scheme again—get my revenge—but I've no longer got an empire to enjoy when it's done."

"Leopard spots, Lucius. *Gorbatovo mogul ispravit.*"

Lucius nodded sagely. "Perhaps I am a hunchback—but while a leopard might not change his spots, Maxine Rider, I've been declawed. I'm not the same animal I once was."

"Perhaps." Maxine said, unconvinced—or at least resisting the urge to become convinced. "All the same, I feel the need to remind you of Vladimir's reach. Although he's no longer running the Russian Mafia, his niece and I *are* acquainted. Any threat to my team, and I'll use her resources to reach you. There are eight Russian immigrants in this prison—any one of which might want to earn favor with the Russian Mafia."

Lucius sighed. "I acknowledge your unveiled threat—and I've

no doubt that you possess the means, the resources, and the balls to carry through with it."

Maxine smirked. "As long as we understand that keeping my people safe takes precedence over any moral quandaries I might face in orchestrating something like that."

"Message received."

Maxine stood, feeling a familiar ache in her knee exacerbated by the long car ride here. Yet, the discomfort was worth the trip to see a man rightfully imprisoned for his crimes and resigned to his fate.

Lucius might yet contemplate a second battle. He had the advantage of time and few distractions. For now, though, it seemed like Maxine had bought the Rider team peace.

THREE MONTHS LATER

Drake watched Claire walk down the aisle in a gleaming, white dress. Her black hair was smoothly pinned back from her lovely face. Thin straps hung on her otherwise bare shoulders. Rhinestones accentuated the low V-neck at the top of the dress. The trumpet design flowed over her hips, before flaring down over the curve of her legs. She looked like a princess—his Princess Andromeda—and Claire was about to have her castle wedding.

Beside her walked Ryan Walsh, escorting her down the aisle. His tuxedo stretched over his broad shoulders. Ryan's wife, Jenna, stood at the altar with the other bridesmaids—Billy, another Rider family member, Aurora, Mason's wife, and Natasha—Vladimir's niece. They all wore teal gowns with gold sequins, which shimmered in the light like dragonfly wings.

Claire had prepped Drake on the entire wedding party so he could try to keep everyone straight. The groomsmen were Pete, Ryan, Reece, and Mason. Poor Pete looked so scrawny in his penguin suite, standing beside two former Rangers and a former Navy Seal. Drake had been relieved his friend had agreed to come to his wedding, after his initially less-than-warm welcome by the Rider team.

As Claire neared the altar, she smiled, setting Drake's world alight. Her expression gleamed with sheer devotion—given without reservation. He belonged to this beautiful woman, heart and soul.

When Claire reached Drake's side, Ryan released her and joined the other groomsmen. Drake took her hand in his and smiled, gazing deeply into her eyes.

He looked spectacularly mouthwatering in his tuxedo. Drake was Claire's Perseus—and together, they'd defeated the Titan— the Kraken. Together, they'd conquer the next demon to cross their path as well.

The two of them turned to watch Mica walk down the aisle with her father. Her gold curls shone glamorously beneath her veil. She wore a white, silk column gown with bare shoulders. Beside Claire, David shifted his weight.

Claire had been surprised when Mica had suggested a joint wedding. Mica might have simply been her ever-practical self— because she'd known they'd have nearly identical guest lists—but Claire had actually loved the idea, envisioning the magic of sharing this special day with Mica, and all of the picture-perfect photos that would result from having a dual wedding. Perhaps, Maxine would also shed fewer tears if they kept their ceremonies contained to a single event.

Claire beamed at Maxine, sitting in the front row beside Vladimir. Maxine rocked the baby seat beside her, which contained Aurora and Mason's sleeping three-month old.

Remarkably, Claire hadn't seen her former boss since Maxine's elopement to Antigua with Vladimir. She was looked tan and healthy now, wearing an elegant purple dress with her steely eyes glistening with tears. Vladimir held her hand. They'd been enjoying retirement on their tropical paradise, not to mention the anonymity that accompanied it. The two of them deserved it, Claire thought.

With a bubbling excitement, Claire watched Mica reach the altar and stand beside David. Her eyes swept the room one last time, drinking in the sight of its grey, stone walls, arching ceiling, blooming geraniums, and the sun streaming through the stained-glass window. Every aspect of this day was picture-perfect—including the family and unity the Rider team had created.

Claire turned to Drake, looking deeply into his eyes as he smiled at her with heart-warming devotion. She knew she'd love this man without reservation—forever.

<<<<>>>>

DEAR READER

If you enjoyed this book and want to know about future releases by CB Samet you can CLICK HERE to sign up for my mailing list! I promise I won't spam you. I only send an email when I have a new book released, giveaways, or special discounts. And I'll never sell your information. You can also unsubscribe at any time.

Also, as an independent author, I rely heavily on readers to spread the word about books they've read. If you enjoyed this story, kindly let others know by posing a brief comment on social media or leave a review where you purchased it.

Click below to follow me on Bookbub!

Thank you for reading,
CB Samet
www.cbsamet.com

ALSO BY CB SAMET

The Rider Files:

Meridian File, Book 1

Masters File, Book 2

McMillan File, Book 3

Maltisse File, Book 4

The Dr. Whyte Series:

Black Gold

Whyte Knight

Gray Horizon

Romancing the Spirit Series

Sadie's Spirit

Willow's Windfall

Cassie's Chase

Phoebe's Pharaoh

Vanessa's Valentine

Like strong women in fantasy?

Check out this great series!

ACKNOWLEDGMENTS

This series would not have been possible without the support of so many people. My husband, first and foremost, helped me brainstorm the plots of each Rider Files (and the ones to come!). He supported me with the time and encouragement I needed to write. My mom has also been supportive of my writing and read all of my books early in their creation. I also have other beta readers who took the time to read and provide feedback.

Next, is my team of professionals. I have a fantastic editor who always adds a layer of polish. The book cover designer for this series created some breath-taking covers I never tire of looking at.

Lastly, are my readers. My review team takes the time and effort to comment on the quality of my work so that new readers will find me. Other readers take a chance on a writer new to them and dive whole-heartedly into the series.

www.ingramcontent.com/pod-product-compliance
Lightning Source LLC
Chambersburg PA
CBHW050508190726
48284CB00003B/731